My Life as a Mermaid

Apr 2016

My Life as
a Mermaid
and Other Stories

Jen Grow

DZANC BOOKS

5220 Dexter Ann Arbor Rd.
Ann Arbor, MI 48103
www.dzancbooks.org

The characters and events in this book are fictitious. Any similarity to real persons, living or dead, is coincidental and not intended by the author.

Designed by Steven Seighman

Library of Congress Cataloging-in-Publication Data
Grow, Jen.
[Short stories. Selections]
My life as a mermaid and other stories / Jen Grow.
    pages cm
    ISBN 978-1-938103-03-2
1. Life change events—Fiction. 2. Psychological fiction. I. Title. II. Title: My life as a mermaid.
PS3607.R6786A6 2015 813'.6—dc23
                                            2015000610

ISBN: 978-1-938103-03-2

First U.S. Edition: June 2015

Printed in the United States of America

10 9 8 7 6 5 4 3 2 1

For Mom, my first reader.

For Dad, thanks for showing me the way.

Table of Contents

My Life as a Mermaid

I get another letter from my sister who is in Honduras riding mules and skidding around the muddy mountain roads in a pickup truck. The roads have curves sharp enough to invite death, sharp enough to see yourself leaving. When the priest drives, she writes, he is the real danger, his faith too strong to be cautious. My sister, Kay, has learned to hope for days when the truck breaks down. Otherwise, she and the other relief workers cower in the open bed as the priest speeds through the countryside; they lean all their weight toward the mountain to keep the truck from sliding off the washed-out roads. Some days they leave their base camp and carry their supplies up the mountains by foot. They pack Tylenol, Imodium, vitamins. And antibiotics: Keflex, Pen-VK, Erythromycin, Lorabid, Roxar, tubes of anti-fungal cream, and everything for parasites.

Me, I stock up on Band-Aids and Flintstones chewables as I wheel my cart down the pharmacy aisle. Suntan lotion, cotton balls, hairspray, toothpaste. I gather toilet paper and paper towels—the jumbo pack—for all the spills I wipe. *Would a sponge work better, save some trees?* my sister might ask. But I am one to leave the sponge in the sink, smelly and sour, until the odor clings to my hands and infects everything I try to clean. "That wouldn't happen if you squeezed it out every time," my husband instructs all of us, the kids included. He demonstrates his method over the sink, a surplus of gray water drizzling from the sponge, an army of germs exterminated. "Squeeze out all the extra," he says. I nod. The kids have lost interest. Still, I prefer paper towels. They absorb everything. Plus, there's the satisfaction of throwing them out—the illusion of messes going away.

In her letter, Kay says there's no indoor plumbing. No showers, no tubs. Toilets that do not flush "as you know it," she says, to emphasize the differences between us. On the other hand, she says, there is plenty of water. It rains daily for an hour or more. She washes in a pan of rainwater, one leg at a time, and keeps her bar of soap, gray and shrinking, in a Ziploc baggie. The Ziploc has become valuable, irreplaceable, and she folds it neatly to preserve it.

When her team of eight (the priest, a couple of saints, a paramedic, a skittish med student, and a teenage interpreter, plus bodyguards strapped in bullets) hikes back, exhausted from a day in the mountains, a day of shouting *"Atención! Atención!"* through a bullhorn to the trees, announcing the arrival of *"medico"* to treat infected hands and swollen limbs that should be amputated, diarrhea of all types, pneumonia, chicken pox, dengue, skin fungus, worms, and clogged ears—when she's finished distributing whatever antibiotics are left to treat the sexual diseases and parasites buried deep within the bodies of these people, my sister carries her bucket of rainwater to her stucco cell, where she soaps herself a leg at a time, an arm, a shoulder, trying to remove the day's dust and sorrow. The stench of sulfur water is not much better than the decay she's wiping clean.

Afterward, she gathers her clothes and scrubs and wrings them in her bathwater and hangs them to dry. Then she uses the twice-dirty water to flush her toilet in the corner of her cell.

She says she has not yet gotten used to the sourness that consumes her hair and skin and clothes. "How does a thing become so soiled? So black and unwanting of touch?" she asked in her letter. I don't know if she is referring to her cell or toilet or the countryside in general. I cannot answer, having never witnessed a thing so dirty as to be mourned.

Many years ago, we were two girls swimming in the ocean every summer. Family vacations, sand and sunburn, salty waves. If not the ocean, we swam in the pool until our lips turned blue. We knew how to make our bodies float or sink, how to dive away from our mother's voice when she pleaded with us to get out. "Girls!" she'd yell. "Girls, I'm warning you, if I have to pull you out myself!" Kay and I would plunge even deeper and isolate ourselves in the silence of the water. We taught ourselves to jump waves, to dive, to hold tea parties underwater until our bodies floated upward and our lungs ran out of air.

I have tried to teach this trick to my own children along with underwater handstands and somersaults, but my children do not swim like me. They have inherited their father's fear. They keep to the shallow end and drift to the sides. My youngest child is afraid to get his face wet, a screamer if he is splashed, hyperventilating until his face is red and purple. When this happens, I hold him close to my chest and gently glide back and forth in the water. But this has never soothed him as it does me. He is most happy playing on the grass, where his feet feel sure of the world beneath him.

There are other children at the community pool who dive deep and search the bottom. Their parents call them fish or mermaids. Lovely swimmers. But they do not belong to me.

On sunny afternoons in my suburban home I worry about my kids, my sister, the world. I fear catastrophe. I'd like to write Kay and ask her how she escaped these worries, but instead I write short letters begging her to be careful. Then I forget to mail them and use the envelopes as a place to jot down my list of things to do:

> *go to post office/bank*
> *laundry*
> *call therapist*
> *get aspirin, ice cream, Diet Coke*
> *nap*

I fuss over my children in the same distracted, heartsick way while I count the tiny pairs of socks that come out of the dryer. I fold their miniature clothes into piles. Some days I feel like Gulliver, every part of me tied down by Lilliputians, as if, somehow, it is me and not my sister who has wandered into a strange land. The land of marriage, motherhood, matching socks. It's not what I expected. How did I choose this, wandering the grocery store with my squeaky cart? Nor is it clear how my sister escaped to Honduras. It seems impossible that all these worlds are connected, the past with the present, Honduras with here. Though in some ways, it could be as simple as purchasing an airline ticket and trusting the winds of God—the whims of God—to land in a small pocket between the slopes of two mountains, like finding shelter between the breasts of a giant mother.

Kay flew to Honduras after a devastating hurricane ripped through the country. The hospital in Tegucigalpa was flooded four stories high. Rushing water sucked bodies away from the villages, depositing death everywhere like sediment. I know this not from the news, which focused on wealthier parts of the world, but from my sister and her small band of relief workers. They flew into a smelly tropical world for various reasons, among them compassion and the longing for a place to hide.

Kay writes, "I took a rare dip in one of the rivers today, surrounded by mangrove trees. I floated in smooth brown water where I wanted to live forever as a fish." I'm envious. I would run away; I would like to be the kind of person who could run away.

Some days I feel like I am at the bottom of an empty aquarium watching the world through a glass wall. The floor of my aquarium is covered with toys that have fallen apart or have missing pieces. "Somebody has to clean this up!" I yell to my children, who are upstairs in their rooms hiding from my voice. When no one comes, I bend down and straighten the mess myself. Pick up the pieces and put them in a pile.

I ask, How on earth can I, from here, straighten up the world? Absorb all the spills? Know in some concrete way how wasteful my wanting is? Every few weeks, I write out another twenty-dollar check to Unicef or the Fireman's Fund, the Police Youth camp, the world food bank. I stuff my checks into their pre-addressed envelopes and then I forget to mail them.

"Don't you think we could do something?" I say to my husband at night in bed. I sound like one of the children pleading to keep a stray kitten.

"You're suffering from guilt," my husband tells me. "Did you call your therapist?"

It's not guilt, I want to explain. *It's something else.* But my husband is a giant wall of a man whose back is turned to me. I draw invisible circles on his skin.

"Go ahead and deny yourself," he says. "But not the rest of us." He's fed up with the diet of rice and onions I've been serving for dinner lately.

"This is what your *Aunt Kay* is eating tonight, so lick your bowls!" I tell the kids. They love the idea of eating with their fingers. "In other parts of the world people are starving," I remind them when they spit out the onions.

"We are civilized in this household. We will use forks," my husband says, too late to stop the chaos at the dinner table.

"What about pizza, Daddy?" one of the kids asks. "We eat that with our hands."

All of us except my husband scoop rice with our fingers, we lick and gobble like the dogs we are. This is play for the children, not a state of being. I cannot replicate the poverty of the world so anyone will believe me, fold hunger back on itself. I cannot pretend I am anywhere but here. We eat mangoes and bananas for dessert. Ice cream. The kids think life's a picnic because we've been eating off paper plates. Since the drought this summer and the state's call to conserve, I've stopped doing dishes. We haven't hooked the hose to the lawn sprinkler, washed the cars, or turned on the birdbath fountain for weeks. My husband thinks this is enough sacrifice. Every evening, he studies the landscaping, which cost a fortune, and the browning lawn. Then he looks at the sky, waiting. I've been making the children bathe at the same time. Three at once is harder to handle, all the splashing and name-calling, the middle child squished in between. After their baths, we scoop the tub water into pots and carry the containers downstairs to soak the houseplants. We drip all the way to the herb garden out back and make circles of mud around the wildflowers and tomato plants. My clean-scrubbed kids parade in their pajamas; gray water the color of old soap dripping down their arms. Really, there is more dirty water than I know what to do with.

I tell them I'm going to the store to buy jugs of water, that I will be back soon. I buy ice cream instead. I buy ice cream regularly these last few months, and each time I drive a little bit farther, looking for a different store, another flavor. We've hoarded several cartons of ice cream at home, gallons of water, so it isn't a need I'm chasing. Water is just my flimsy excuse to get away. Lately, I've been taking refuge in the grocery store. I wheel up and down the aisles, amazed by the abundance. I study the shelves of canned vegetables, rows of soup. "Excuse me," I hear a woman ask the clerk. "Can you tell me where to find artichokes?" She pronounces it *"heart-a-choke,"* and I think, "They're everywhere. Poor choking hearts." For instance, this one: Kay wrote me about a woman with mastitis. The woman had a giant sloughing pit of a breast, a hollow where her body used to be. The worst case Kay's ever seen. I cannot picture it, except as black ash. A side of a woman ready to blow away.

Tonight, I finger the fresh produce. I stop my cart next to a bin of corn on the cob and pick out an ear. I pull back the husk and part the silk—the kids call it Barbie hair. They love to play with corn silk Barbie. Beautiful Barbie. Except squirming underneath the Barbie hair is a fat worm tunneling its way through the ear of corn. Even the worms of this country eat well. I think of the Honduran children Kay wrote about, some of whom had worms sprouting from their foreheads. The *torsala* flies that are everywhere in Honduras circle the children's heads like black halos. When the children are napping, the flies bite their foreheads and lay eggs. The larvae hatch from swollen pouches. Kay says it's a horrific sight, but not life-threatening, easy enough to treat with antibiotics and creams. How can worms bursting from a child's forehead not be threatening to life? To my life? I am haunted by these images when I bathe my children at night, their skin glowing gorgeous, as smooth as perfect fresh peaches, which, I notice, are on sale. I pick out a half-dozen flawless fruits and admire the beauty of things grown without deformities.

At night, when I count my children and make sure all are safe and sleeping, when I lie in bed with my husband and stare at his back, I think of letters I'll write my sister. "When you are taking care of other people's children," I'll ask her, "who do you count as belonging to you?"

I leave the grocery store with a gallon of water, a carton of ice cream, the peaches, and a bundle of paper towels. Weaving through the parking lot, I see myself in someone's side-view mirror, my hair in my eyes, my French twist loose and lopsided, my arm stretched around the jumbo paper towels. I balance them on my hip as if I am carrying one more child, the child who will clean up the world, wipe up the spills, absorb it all.

I carry my groceries through the parking lot, and then, before I move in time, an old woman backs her car into my hip. "Hey!" I yell. I pound my fist on her trunk and drop my bags. She's wearing a feathered hat and cannot fully turn her neck to see me. "Is that a condition of old age or of life—the not turning to see?" I want to ask. But the peaches are rolling across the asphalt, and the plastic jug has split. Clean, clear water seeps from the burst seam, forming small puddles and soaking the pavement like a stain. I can see the old woman's hands tremble on the steering wheel. She must be somebody's mother. I can tell she would like to help me pick up my groceries but doesn't know how. She cannot move from inside the safe bubble of her car except to wave and say she's sorry.

Joe Blow

Larry and Roger live in this abandoned truck like kings, like they own the thing. They bounce on the springs and pass out against the windows while the whole cab gets smelly and fogged with their breath. They sit in the truck all day like they're at the drive-in matinee, unaffected by the movie of life. They watch the rest of us through the birdshit windshield and pass their bottle back and forth as casually as if they're sharing popcorn.

We ignore them mostly. We say, "Hey! Larry! Don't throw your bottles on the street!"

He shakes his head. "It wasn't me. Musta been one of those kids."

And we go, "Yeah, right."

But pretty soon, no more bottles on the street, they're in the back of the pickup. We might mention the cigarette butts, too, but that doesn't change. Little brown and white filters all over the place, like confetti. The more important thing is the broken glass. So now that's OK. No more flats. Larry and Roger understand the courtesy of this, even if their tires don't roll anywhere.

Behind the glass windshield, they forget that we can see them. They watch the neighborhood like drunken sentinels. They wait for the mail lady, hope for their SSI checks, ward off stray dogs and the weather. When it's cold, they huddle in the cab of the truck, don't move, don't talk, tuck their hands under their armpits. "Winter is the bastard who beats his wife," we heard Larry mumble through the glass one day. Surprised, we looked up from the sidewalk. Did he really say that, or did he say something else? It's like the first line of a poem he never finished.

When spring comes and the air is warmer, Larry and Roger climb out of the truck and sit on the front stoop of Carl's row house. The two men are like cats, the way they soak in the sun—cats without the preening. Carl the pill dealer lets them sit there while he obsessively polishes his car. Every day, it seems, he's out there waxing and polishing his orange GTO with the talking alarm. He revs the engine the way another man would flex his muscles. Tina, the pill dealer's daughter, thin as a butterfly, flits in circles as she talks to Larry and plays games.

"What's the capital of Kansas?" she asks.

"Kansas City," Larry answers. It's amazing what he knows.

Tina is not afraid of Larry, of how he looks or smells, or the pee stains that grow underneath him on the steps. All the years of her life he has lived outside on her street. She knows him like she knows her dog. Loves them in the same way.

Carl the pill dealer jokes with Larry and Roger, buys them sodas every so often, or fries. We've seen him bend over a boat of French fries on Roger's lap and squirt catsup because Roger's hands are too shaky to handle the packets. Carl the pill dealer goes, "Now share," and leaves Tina on the steps with Roger and Larry, who are like her uncle and grandfather, sort of.

Tina plays hopscotch and asks them questions. "What color am I thinking of?" she quizzes them.

"White."

"What?" she squeals. "That's not it!"

Sometimes their conversations are more searching. We've seen her look to the sky and point. Larry nods and points too. He's explaining something to her. The birds? The clouds? God knows.

No one asks questions when Carl comes home a few hours later with a bandage on his ear. Sometimes he's got a big white bandage on the side of his head like an East Baltimore Van Gogh, one who'd cut off his ear for the obsessive love of his car, the anguish of birdshit on his polished hood. We all know the bandages mean someone's punched him in his bad ear again.

"Don't lean on my car!" Carl warns Larry and Roger when they stumble across the street to spend the night in their truck.

Other days we've seen the neighborhood boys stand outside of Larry and Roger's truck, calling them names and throwing tiny pebbles and handfuls of dirt at the truck.

"Cut it out, you little motherfuckers!" Larry yells at them. He would throw stones back, but he can't get out of the truck or bend over without falling on his head.

"They're throwing things at us," Larry says as we pass by. He says it like he's ten years old.

A pebble the size of a grain of rice bounces off the truck.

"I'll whup your asses!" Larry yells, unable to defend himself any other way. His eyes are red with the fury of another lost fight. The kids snicker.

"See what I mean?" Larry insists. "They started it."

Except for the kids, most everyone forgets to notice Larry and Roger. It's like if you lived in a place with mountains in the background: every day of seeing mountains, they wouldn't seem so large anymore, just ordinary, and pretty soon you'd forget to notice them. You'd become bored. That's how we get with the trash on the street. That's how we get with Larry and Roger.

Then Joe moves into the neighborhood and starts with the broom. Up and down both sides of the street, going everywhere with his trashcan on wheels. Sweeping the sidewalk, the curb, trying to get every last one of those cigarette butts. Impossible, when the filters keep multiplying. He ignores the dogs in the alley that bark and yap at him as he pushes his broom.

Soon, Joe starts pounding on his house. We find out he's a carpenter, a rehabber. Before he moved here, he renovated another house a few blocks away in Butcher's Hill, an old German row house on Pratt Street that once belonged to a family of brewers. Which family? Which brewery? "At one time, this was the neighborhood for beer!" Joe says. He's read up on it, has a yellowed piece of paper that shows a picture of his former house as it looked in the 1920s. The caption reads, "F. Scott Fitzgerald was known to visit this home with other writers and thinkers." At every opportunity, Joe shows us this article. He unfolds his wallet and pulls the newsprint from its slot.

"Let me see," Larry calls out from the truck. The truck is parked in front of Joe's row house, where Larry and Roger can see and hear everything. Joe hesitates, then walks halfway to the cab window and holds the article carefully out of Larry's reach.

"I can't read that. My eyes are wobbling," Larry complains. His eyes are usually some shade of bloodshot. Roger just nods. He's wearing a pair of boxy glaucoma sunglasses he found on the street.

"It says F. Scott Fitzgerald used to visit the house where I lived," Joe tells them.

"Where's that?" Larry asks. "Across from that old lesbian bar?" Roger laughs.

Joe eyeballs both of them, folds his paper in his wallet, and turns toward the rest of us.

It's true. The neighborhood isn't grand anymore. The old homes with marble steps have been hacked into apartments. Across from the house that used to be Joe's, the house that used to welcome writers and thinkers, sits a sad, empty lesbian bar in a building that used to be something else. Everything around us used to be something else.

"That Fitzgerald was some alcoholic," Larry says with a sneer, as if he can hold Joe in the same contempt. An ambulance blows by, its siren blaring, and drowns out Larry's voice. His mouth moves, but we can't hear him.

The next thing Joe does is fashion a long pole with a cutter at the end to snip the blue plastic bags from the trees. Snip, snip—down floats a bag like a long-lost balloon. Joe stuffs the bag in a sack with the other bags he's collected, like he's picking withered berries.

"It's a w-waste of t-t-time," the stuttering man dismisses Joe. The stuttering man lives with his mother, who wants to move out of Baltimore; she's put her house up for sale, but so far, no luck. "The trash just b-bl-blows in again," he says while Joe balances his aluminum pole in the air. He's concentrating on a knotted bag near the top of the linden tree. The stuttering man shakes his head. He doesn't like Joe, but he lets him sweep in front of his mother's house, cut down bags. "A little more to the l-left," he directs from his screen door.

"To the right!" Larry yells from the truck. The stuttering man doesn't like Larry or Roger, either.

Roger doesn't have an opinion. He's pressed into the corner of the truck, boxed in by his giant sunglasses and his bright orange cap. It's like he's trying to hide from our sight, hide from Joe. Roger forgets his cap is so loud orange. His cap is louder than he is.

But Larry talks to everyone. He's made friends with the mail lady. He calls her Babycakes. "How're you doin', Babycakes?" he asks. The mail lady is friendly, but not too good with the house numbers. She keeps a pint in her bag and stops to take a little nip with Larry almost every morning. She pours some into a cup for him, and they toast. "Gotta go now, Larry. Look at all this mail. My feet are killing me," she says, "and it's only nine o'clock in the morning."

"Tell me about it," Larry starts.

Larry's got stories about his feet. They puff out of his boots. It's not just Larry's drunkenness that keeps him from walking straight. His feet are swollen, which, according to the street doctors, is a bad sign. Bad like drawing the wrong upside-down card from the fortuneteller, something that means death. It's a hush, though—no one will say it out loud.

Somebody gave Larry crutches. He might as well be walking on stilts, as clumsy as he is. There's a skinny guy in a bandana who sometimes helps Larry cross the street to the liquor store. The bandana guy helps Roger, too, who doesn't have foot problems, except when he's too drunk to walk. We've seen this from the window: the bandana guy steadying them, one at a time, his arm tight around the waist like he's strolling with his granny. Two drunk, weak, stumbling Grandmas, one named Larry, one named Roger. The bandana guy is as gentle as he's ever going to get when he tucks the drunks into their cab to pass out. Because, other than that, he spends a lot of time shouting at his girlfriend.

"You're an idiot!"

"I hate you!"

Every Saturday night.

Dogs bark in the alley. Somebody blares rap from his car stereo till the base vibrates the windows. Meanwhile, Joe builds flower boxes and starts calling the cops.

The police get to know Larry and Roger on a first-name basis. When the squad car drives up, the cops nod to Larry and Roger, tell them to move on. "Move on," they say over the bullhorn, like they're talking to a crowd. "No loitering." Larry makes like he's reaching for his crutches, pretends he's going to stand, and stalls long enough for the squad car to roll away.

A couple of hours later, Joe might call the cops again. The cops drive by, make sure Larry stands all the way up this time; maybe they watch him struggle a few yards on his crutches before they leave. Then Larry sits down and there goes Joe again, on the phone dialing 911. Three or four times a day. It's not long before everyone involved is annoyed. After a while of this, Larry and Roger stay in the truck. The cops can't cite them when they're inside a vehicle. So they sweat out the summer with the windows rolled down. They wait until Joe leaves for work and then scramble outside to catch a breeze.

Linda, our neighbor down the block, goes, "I never thought of it as loitering before. Larry and Roger are just out here, like the lamppost, like the stoplight. I never thought of it as loitering. Roger's parents live around the corner. Larry's wife used to be here. That's not loitering." Linda works for a wholesale place and gives Larry and Roger apples and old produce, which they have a hard time chewing.

But Joe is determined. "Let them go around the corner to Roger's house, then—let them go somewhere else!" He protests not to Linda, but to all of us, to the air.

"Roger's parents don't want him," Linda explains. This is common knowledge, but Joe shakes his head anyway.

Joe is divorced, and the women in the neighborhood can't understand why, as handy as he is, and fully employed. But the men can see the problem clearly. Joe makes all of us look bad; he can't leave well enough alone. His business cards read, "Joe Blozman Home Improvement," like it's part of his name. "Joe Blow," a few people say, not to his face.

"Joe's a *renovator*," Carl tells us snidely. "Let him rehab his own life, leave the rest of us out of it." Carl the pill dealer is uncomfortable with so many uniforms in the neighborhood.

"They can't stay here," Joe insists. We look across the street to where they're sitting, Larry and Roger, propping each other up, both of them bruised with bloody lips from their fight last night over the last drops in the bottle. We've seen it happen plenty of times: Roger is an angry drunk and bigger, so he pushes Larry out of the truck or off the stoop where they're sitting, and Larry can't walk, he falls over like a sack of potatoes, scrapes his face on the sidewalk. But the lust for vodka can make him abnormally strong, and pretty soon, Larry will pull himself up, bad feet and all, and stumble over to Roger. Then they start punching and yelling—"Fuck! Fuck! Fucker!" back and forth, slurring their words, spitting out blood, coughing, until Larry can't move and passes out in a heap and Roger, drunk as he is, stumbles around the corner to beg another bottle.

The next day, they might sit on opposite sides of the street and not talk. Or one of them will stay inside the truck, the other outside. It's like a domestic dispute, which most of us stay out of, won't call the cops for something as ordinary as yelling between a man and his wife.

Maybe the mail lady will come by and share a nip with Larry while he recounts his grievances, how he's angry and proud. He'll sit like a king on a throne, and maybe pee stains will grow beneath him on the cement steps while he pretends he doesn't notice.

Roger doesn't say a word, just tucks his head under that orange hunting cap as if no one can see him. His shame is so big he'd like to hide from it. And still, once a month, he sneaks home, back into his mother's heart, begging for money or some food. When he slips through the alley, the dogs in the neighborhood growl and jump against their chain-link fences.

Soon enough, Roger stumbles across the street to sit beside Larry again. He doesn't make a sound while Larry holds court with Carl or the bandana man. "I'm fifty-three years old today!" Larry slurs like he's got mush in his mouth.

Roger smiles. We've heard this before; Larry celebrates his fifty-third birthday often.

"I didn't know what else to do," he explains. "I don't have any family. Just this knucklehead," and he elbows Roger, who struggles to keep himself balanced. "All I want is a pretty girl and a million bucks," Larry muses to no one in particular. "Even if I lost them, I could say I had them once."

Carl snorts, but the bandana man nods. Roger takes a swig from the bottle. Latin music blares out a window from somebody's radio. "Turn it down!" the bandana man yells. Everyone is quiet a minute while Larry thinks.

"There's something else I want, but I can't remember what it is."

The other thing that happens: Joe calls the city about having the abandoned truck towed.

First, the cops stick a couple of tickets on the windshield every few days. The tickets collect under the folded arms of the windshield wipers. They flap in the breeze, get soggy with rain. It's September; the color of the sun has changed, the leaves are dark, dark green. Larry and Roger haven't noticed them.

Then, maybe a month later, a tow truck pulls up. It makes noise as it idles and the radio plays. Yellow lights radiate in a circle on top of the truck. A man in a clean t-shirt gets out. He bends on one knee, and looks underneath Larry and Roger's truck, inspects it, pulls on something.

Larry and Roger are across the street soaking in the last rays of Indian summer. They've got their wine goggles on and can't see straight, can't see clearly to the other side of the block.

"Hey, isn't that your truck?" somebody says as they pass. "Are they taking your truck?"

"What?" Larry says. Roger puffs up.

Somebody's dog barks from a window, scratches at the glass.

Joe opens his front door and watches the tow truck from his stoop. The stuttering man opens his screen door and watches, too.

"Hey!" Larry yells. He struggles to find his crutches, leans heavily on them but cannot pull himself up.

"Hey!" Roger echoes. "Hey, you!" Roger is having foot problems because he is too drunk.

"Hey, you! Get off!" Larry yells.

We open our windows at the commotion, lean outside to watch. The tow truck man lowers some chains and cables that clank on the pavement. He places two brackets behind Larry and Roger's truck wheels, inserts steel pins to keep the truck in place. Then he jumps back into the tow truck for the controls. He flips a switch. We hear some gears grind, and then the hydraulic motor makes a loud whirring noise as Larry and Roger's truck slowly rises. The sound expands, reverberating off the row houses in the neighborhood.

"You're doing fine," Joe yells to the tow truck man. But the tow truck man doesn't hear, or pretends he doesn't hear. He's got a clipboard with paperwork that he checks off as the abandoned truck lifts higher.

"I'm telling you to get off!" Larry yells. But the sound of the tow truck is so loud, no one can hear him. He is up and wobbling on his crutches, trying to pitch forward into a walk.

"Motherfucker, get off our truck!" Roger yells. This might be the first full sentence we've heard Roger say in a long time.

"Do you want me to call the police?" Joe yells to the tow truck man. The tow truck man shakes his head.

"Stop!" Roger screams. It's a high-pitched wail, really. His vocal chords stretch with the effort. Tears are in his eyes. He grabs the trunk of the linden tree and holds on for balance, holds on for life as if he is being swept away by a flash flood. He rubs his face against the bark, then starts banging his forehead. He knocks his skull on the tree, harder and harder, like he's trying to shake something loose inside himself. "Don't! Don't! Don't!" he cries to himself and everyone else.

Then he looks up. "Motherfucker!" he screams. "Stop taking our truck!"

"Oh sh-shut up," the stuttering man dismisses him. No one hears the stuttering man except us.

When Larry and Roger's truck is secured, the hydraulic noise stops. The tow truck man gets back into the cab of his truck and shifts gears again.

Larry is quiet. Stooped over his crutches, he stands as straight as he ever will. He watches the tow truck pull away. "God help me," we think we hear him say. Did he say that, or did he say something else? We know this much: Larry is used to losing, has lost everything. Does he cry when his truck is towed? We can't tell. He just watches the tires roll down the street and stop when the truck reaches the next red light. Larry waits. His bottle is firm in his hand.

But Roger is younger and righteous. "Joe, you pussy!" he yells. His face is red. He bangs his head on the tree again, scraping his cheek on the bark. Spit forms at the corner of his mouth. He's like a rabid dog. There are large welts on his face. He tries to kick the tree and misses. He loses his balance and wraps both arms around the tree as he falls, hugs the trunk like he's clinging to his mother's leg.

"Joe! You fucking coward!" he yells. His anger is all he has.

"He was only doing his job!" Joe yells back.

"You're a coward!" Roger bellows. He's on the ground, throwing handfuls of dirt towards Joe's side of the street.

We shake our heads at the scene below. From our sidewalks and front doors and from our second-floor windows, we see all. Like God, almost. There's Joe, there's Roger, opposite sides of the street, hating something about each other. And the tow truck in the middle, waiting at the end of the block for the light to change to green. We could spit on Larry if we wanted to. Hock a lugie on Joe. But when the light turns green, all of us watch quietly as the tow truck makes a turn around the corner and drives out of sight.

"That's the cause and effect of it," we might say, and pull our heads inside. We're tired of the circus, but we keep the window open for a breeze, maybe prop it up with a stick or a ruler, an empty beer can.

Who knows who's right? Larry and Roger live here, too. But when Joe Blow moves in across the street, he goes everywhere with his broom and his trashcan on wheels. The neighborhood eventually gets better, years later, but we don't know that yet.

What Girls Leave Behind

Pink plastic pearls from a broken elastic bracelet. Like these I'm holding between my fingers. Pretend jewels, or princess dreams fallen apart. I still find them, left over from years ago, pill-sized shocks of truth. These silly reminders of what little girls are like—this is what makes me start thinking again. I imagine all those beads rolling away, like refugees, scurrying to places small and safe, away from a vacuum.

How did the rubber band snap? I don't remember, but I can picture it in my head. Hear it. All the confusion, a swirl, a smash. Noisy girls running in my apartment, my daughters on visitation. Afterward, a string of things left behind: purple socks and stains, a fuzzy blue bumblebee and soggy pretzel sticks, plastic juice cups half filled with red Kool-Aid.

Those nights, weekends—when sometimes I was drunk and sometimes I was angry—are caught in the amber of black-outs and scotch. My memory has condensed the years into slow-moving stick-figure cartoons, the kind we drew when we were kids, the barest outlines of motion. Occasionally I remember a startling fragment that makes me jump as if a bug has flown in my mouth and is caught in my throat. I'm terrified of swallowing.

But this comes back to me: a moment one evening, an undrunk feeling. I was boiling frozen corn for dinner and drinking scotch when an unclouded notion of myself bubbled up in the boiling water. I was a wilting woman, a drunk, slicing the corner of a plastic bag and pouring frozen kernels into a pan on the stove. This is who I am, I thought. Wilt, wilting, being wilted.

(Or this: Wilt disease, a highly infectious disease of some caterpillars in which the carcasses liquefy. I learned this from the glossy pages of the *World of Insects*, an elementary encyclopedia the girls left here.)

Maybe something else washed by. A sense that there were layers to this existence, invisible but real: that some larger life was taking place in my own living room, where the girls played Barbies and sang and painted. The *living* room! A place I couldn't see from the kitchen. "Something is going on here," I said to the corn. Then it passed. I gulped my scotch and called them to dinner.

"Sit at the table!" I yelled too loudly. Everything was a chore of impossible weight. Getting all the cooking finished at the same time, for instance. And then, having the girls sit down simultaneously. We'd eat. Yellow, red, brown, the color of dinner: corn, catsup, fish sticks. Or else I'd sneak home leftovers from the caterer where I worked. Crab dip and a couple of slices of somebody's wedding cake for dessert.

"I'm a good mother. I'm a very good mother, just tired right now," is how you lie in your head.

The girls would leave purple magic markers around the house, and bobby pins, white underwear with violets and bows, wet bathing suits peeled off in a hurry, stuffed bears and monkeys, and pillow cases, and glass jars with dead bugs, and tears, and love notes, and baby teeth, and fear of jumping from the diving board. I taught them to dive one summer, how to jump in head first. Those were good days.

I remember this as I crawl on my hands and knees, a sad animal, feeling about in dark corners for old toys and beads and other things I've forgotten. It's late afternoon and the sun is weak through the blinds. I want to find more pink pearls. I want to see my girls young again. Because I had not been paying attention, or else I'd been hearing and seeing the wrong things. I miss them, *missed* them while they were jumping around the house and squeaking and playing and crying and splashing each other in the bathtub. I can hear it, the swoosh and slap of water against the sides of the tub. I can hear that with my hand.

Some days I was sick and couldn't lift my head from the pillow, and some days I was moody and strong, the wrong side of a storm.

They'd play games with each other: "You be the vampire this time, but NO biting."

"OK." Then, two minutes later, a scream.

"Ouch! Stop it!" One of them crying out, usually Missy, the oldest. "You don't play right!"

"I'm sorry," Janine would answer in a baby voice, too late for the fat rubber band snap of my patience. A broken band stinging the skin, that was my voice, the belt of my unpredictable anger.

(When I was pregnant, no one ever told me—no one ever touched my elbow and pulled me aside and said, "I just want to tell you this. Children are hard." Which is what I would say, now, if anyone asked.)

Believe me. I painted pictures with them, and we'd laugh and pull out fancy clothes and hats. We played dress-up with my shoes and slips and lipstick. My baby walked around with pantyhose on her head like long, floppy ears. We wore gloves—I had a box full of gloves, soft, flat palms. The girls would pull out more and more of my clothes until I got tired. "That's enough," I'd announce before they were through. Suddenly I wouldn't have the energy to move.

"Hey!" I'd frown and snap my fingers. I used to sit in a corner of the room with my back propped against the wall and drink scotch from my favorite glass.

"Don't run! Don't walk down the steps in my high heels!" Because someone always falls, someone *always* gets hurt. "Put. It. Down!" I'd yell when they were shoving each other and bickering over the same hat. My hand coming down hard and flat on a tabletop. My eyes humorless and mean, my mouth a tight line. There are not too many pictures of me smiling. I didn't like my teeth showing.

I still don't smile much, I realize, as I sit in the corner of my room, my back propped up against the wall, a bottle within reach. I hold a box of photographs on my lap and narrate. "Here's one of me holding my daughter when she was a baby, my first," I say. "Well, no, actually, that might be my second. And here's this one, I was so young. This is of me and my ex-husband when we got married. Look how smooth my skin was. This was taken on our wedding day. I mean, we look dumb, smiling like that. No idea what was coming." I pretend I'm showing my daughters or my mother or the woman down the street who walks her boy to school.

"Look here," I say to none of them. "The photographer posed us near the doors, and next to us is the church suggestion box. See that?" I point. "Suggestion box in our wedding picture. Ha!" I've often wondered, for years, what little pieces of paper were jammed inside, what kind of advice? Maybe something like: These two people shouldn't get married. Or have children. Or drink.

"For the record, I am not the only one who fucked up," I explain to the photographs. But no one answers to say, "Yes, I know."

In theory, I got married when I was seventeen so I could move to California. My husband, who was just a kid when I think about it, promised to take me as far away from my mother as possible. Get all the way away. As it turns out, all we did was move to the other side of Baltimore.

We were so naive, so full of expectations. Once, soon after we were married, we drove up to Pennsylvania. My husband was going to treat us to a weekend away in the mountains. I wore a brand-new wool dress. The first time in my life I was really going somewhere. It snowed tiny flurries as we left the city, small, gray strays that would never amount to anything. ("You will never amount to anything!" my mother used to hiss. She was the smeary picture of gin. To this day, I don't drink it.) As we drove farther north, half an hour, the snowflakes kept falling, more and faster, until we had to turn around and come home. We never even left the state.

I remember snow blindness and silence on the drive back, a kind of deafness. My husband was concentrating so hard, his knuckles were white on the steering wheel. I felt burning needles in my toes because the car heater didn't work. "There's nothing to cry about," he said. So I stared out the window, trapped and disappointed, angry, cold. This is how I took my first few drinks, to take the chill out of life.

I used to make our bed every morning and cook dinner when I got home from my job as a doctor's receptionist. He was good to me; he'd give me pills for my nerves. My husband had a job too, selling rivets or something, and every night he'd recite his plans for us. "After we have our first kid, we'll move into a bigger house," he'd say, as if it was foolproof. His grip was on everything: he had the mortgage worked out, the car payments, the timing of my pregnancies. He picked out what clothes I should wear, the food we'd eat, the friends I should make. I lived in a glass jar with holes poked in the lid for air.

My ex-husband is a piece of work. I don't even like saying his name, stuck with it as I am. He used to wear a gold cross around his neck like a saint, like someone who is never wrong. Most of the time he walked around shirtless, as if he were Atlas, so busy holding up our world. Why did he have to squeeze it to death? To plan every move? That's like trying to figure what path a tear will take down your face. Maybe it gets stuck, maybe it drips off your chin. You don't know. Let me tell you, it's no fun being married to Atlas.

I made friends with the girl next door, Evelyn, who was three years older than me and liked to drink. She had a baby already and lived with this guy who worked where my husband worked, and things were fine. We had cookouts with hotdogs and beer, and we'd laugh. I can still picture the crinkled scar near her eyebrow when she smiled and her fake diamond earrings swinging wildly from her ears. She was always losing them. We wandered the floors of her living room, kitchen, bedroom, the supermarket and liquor store on our hands and knees looking for her earrings. "It's here somewhere," she'd say, and we'd drop to the floor, searching for her worthless jewels. We flirted with everyone. I developed a big laugh. I became friendly with strangers. We spent our afternoons at the corner bar and had fun. She'd leave her infant alone whenever she went out, and I didn't know any better. I was a child myself.

Then she went away and I never saw her again. I felt so alone.

("Ladybug, ladybug, fly away home, your house is on fire, your children are gone." I sang that with the girls when they were old enough to play by themselves in the backyard. They'd dig up worms and pull them apart, save them in a bucket of dirt and wait for the worms to regenerate. One afternoon they found a butterfly struggling to break free of its cocoon. The girls pulled the sack open, but the butterfly struggled and fluttered in circles, heavy and lopsided.)

My husband didn't foresee that I'd become so restless for months afterward, that the dishes would pile up, that something inside me would stop. My heart, maybe. It clicked shut like an iron door.

"It's hard to give a shit these days," I sang to myself like a country-western classic. I still went to the bar.

My husband became outraged and jealous; he'd throw dirty plates against the wall and jerk me by the arm to scold me, grab my hair to keep me still. I got bruises. Some might say, in his defense, it's hard to live with a drunk. For a while, I thought it was love, so I stayed. But inside my head I sang even louder. I made promises and wishes to myself, and then I stopped coming home.

My mother, she used to pull me like that. She left marks. She had long, sharp fingernails the color of tobacco, and she teased her hair. "She doesn't mean it. She's sickly," my aunts told me when I was young. I dreamed I was Dorothy, throwing water on the Wicked Witch and watching her melt.

I don't have any pictures left of myself as a child, but I think my girls look like I did. My baby has my straight, thin hair. If I had different hair, I might be beautiful. "She's cursed with my hair," I say to other mothers, proud in a way that my girl has something of me besides fear. She's got round eyes that smile or cry in a blink. She's a bubble with a round tummy, fat knees with dimples, a red mustache from drinking so much juice. This is how I still see her.

I pull out the next picture and look in the mirror to compare us. "Look at this," I say. "The older one has my sharp nose and the long curve of my eyebrows. She stands just like me, with one hip jutted out, her fragile fist propped on it like a dare." I don't say out loud how she pokes her sister with tense meanness when she's angry. "Where do you think she got that from?" my ex accuses. This child is serious, so serious. Her dark eyes have absorbed every detail, every speck. She has thoughts she will not let go of.

I tried not to say mean things to my girls about their father, but words slipped out. "Girls, your father is a jackass with no poetry in his soul," I sneered a couple of times. After all, I sang to them and read books, while he was as plain as a fact, black-and-white, no nuance, his heart a thick metal square.

"Their father is an unfeeling bastard, a son of a bitch," I say out loud. "He's lied. He's taken my daughters away from me and exaggerates things about me which he refuses to understand. He says I'm a bad influence, that I've left handprints, scars on my daughters. I ask you, what kind of mother would do that?" I'm sitting on the floor, the phone next to me, and I'm talking to a woman, someone I don't know, from an alcoholic hotline I dial when I'm lonely. "But he won't listen. There was a purple bruise on my younger daughter's thigh from when she fell against the table leg. It was an accident. But he's unflinching." After a while I forget she's there, the woman on the phone. I don't hear what she says back to me.

Sometimes I asked the girls questions when I didn't mean to, like: "How's your father's new girlfriend? Is she nice?" Fine, they'd answer. No hints. They were so young and already knew how to keep secrets.

If they were here right this minute, I'd say this: "I apologize for the day you wanted to go swimming and I didn't take you." They would forgive me, I know.

They begged me to take them to the pool. "Teach us how to dive again!" They pleaded with me to put on my bathing suit. "You look fine, Mom," they said, but I didn't like what I saw in the mirror. My stringy hair and slumped shoulders, my stomach bloated from booze. We stayed home while I sat on the end of the sofa and watched my stories and drank. It was a hot, quiet afternoon, dark with the blinds pulled down. They were playing quietly, but somehow my fingernail polish was spilled on the carpet.

"Goddamn, girls!" I screamed, this voice of mine bursting delicate ears like the loudest monster of all dreams. The worst kind. Where does this *voice* come from? "All these spills I have to clean up! Goddamn it!!" I grabbed at something, an arm. I was pulling my older girl at an odd angle from her armpit, dragging, yanking her with my fist. I squeezed harder.

"I *told* you girls *never* to touch anything of mine with*out* asking first! You don't *listen* to *ME*! You *never listen* to *ME*!" These words pounded my girls, pummeled and bruised them until they lost the air to breathe. A force was inside me that had nothing to do with fingernail polish. Thrill and terror. A scream inside my head, and outside, and my ears not recognizing the difference.

"Jesus fucking Christ! Go get a towel!" I said, and let go of her arm. She stood up slowly and put her hand on the sore spot where my fingerprints tattooed her skin. The younger one stood up, too, and they said something to each other with their eyes. There was that millisecond I saw between them. One of them rushed out of the room to get a towel, and the other couldn't look at me: she left, too.

"You need a *wet* towel," I cried when they came back. "A wet towel!"

"I told you," I heard one of them barely breathe to the other. They hurried to leave me.

I slumped to the floor on my knees and swallowed the rest of my scotch. I wanted it so much I could've licked the inside of the glass.

"I tell you this because I need to explain," I say to the photographs, to the images who might be listening. "I heard the only fear we're born with is the fear of loud noises. So I'm sorry. This is how sorry I am."

Sometimes my older girl would follow me around with a pink plastic pail of water because she didn't want me to burn the house down with my cigarettes when I passed out. It wasn't always like that, though. We brushed hair and sang and ate pop-corn and cake for breakfast. We slept on the floor in a huddle underneath our blanket tents when it was cold, when the elec-tricity got turned off. There was the time one of my boyfriends took us to play miniature golf, except the car broke down on the way. He left to find a garage and we sat in the car, waiting for him to come back with a gas can. Long, hot hours, and then it rained. We rolled up the windows and breathed stuffy air and watched giant drops fall on the windshield. "There is nothing to cry about," I said when my baby began to sniffle. Her thumb was in her mouth. Hot tears rolled down her cheeks. We sat in the car on the side of the road like sweaty, dead fish in a dried-out aquarium. A fish tank with all the water on the outside.

After they left me behind, there were spills I couldn't clean up for a few days because they made me too sad to try. Pudding sat in a puddle on the table and made the wood turn white where it seeped through. There was a half-eaten bowl of ice cream turned to soup, hairbrushes and Band-Aids, dinner dishes piled in the sink with dried catsup and crumbs. I had spills of my own, one boyfriend pouring into the next. I made a mess of it. Around me are the remains of all that's been broken, and everything I walk on feels like sharp slivers.

I used to have a favorite glass, sparkling with cut grooves at the base. I sat it down for a second, just one second, on the edge of the table, just long enough for my older daughter, Missy, to knock it off. I can see her in my head. What is she doing? She's swirling and singing. "Mom," Janine is saying, "help me get this unknotted," and she is holding up a shimmering tangle of old necklaces. So I put my glass down for just a second.

Some things, I didn't mind if they got ruined, and some things, they made me mad. My daughters didn't know the difference. So, my glass fell to the floor and a triangle the size of an arrowhead chipped off. I felt like I'd been pierced. Not everything spilled

out, but glass chips floated in the scotch. I couldn't drink it. I had
to pour it out and it broke my heart. I couldn't even yell before I
began to sob. "We're sorry, Mom," they whispered, and their small
hands patted my hair, so light, like careful spiders. Afraid to touch
me. All three of us cried—I will always remember that part. Sitting Indian-style on the floor, and then all of us wiping our noses
on my sweatshirt. I said, "Why are you guys crying?" and they
answered in soft voices, "We don't want you to get mad." I cried
even harder. My girls are quiet when they talk. They're beautiful.

Since then, I get a few weeks here and there. Nine and a half
months, once. Sober. I almost made it. I call those hotline people
on the phone and they do what they can. Remorse follows me
like a cloud. I'll try again one of these days, but I can never stand
the emptiness.

The little girl sounds are gone. I said, "You can't take them
away. I'm their mother." But anyhow. All the paperwork and
lawyers and court dates are a blur. The details mean nothing.

I get school pictures in the mail every year. They've gone
from crooked teeth and straight haircuts when they were seven
and eight to braces and training bras and eyeliner and miniature
bikinis, size two. Then one day it'll be sex too young with some
dumbass boy, and pregnancy, fights and screaming, then divorce
from another SOB, and no children. The silence of that, of children taken away.

What's left is the sound of water dripping. I hear the bus
thunder down the street, an occasional siren, the cats fighting in
the alley, the pipes from the apartment next door, the constant
tick of my alarm clock. Late at night, my eyes open in the dark,
click, click, click, click, click.

"It could be worse," I always say.

The box of pictures is still on my lap, the phone off the hook
next to me. The sun has gone down. I feel around the bottom of
the box and find the remains of an old earring and one last pho-

to, of me and Evelyn, when I was still thin and lovely. We're in our bikinis by the plastic blow-up pool, and my husband is in the background with the garden hose. Evelyn holds her baby and waves like a queen. I'd forgotten this, the end of that summer.

One day we were drinking wine, roaming the bar floor on our hands and knees, laughing and hunting in the dark, under every barstool, for the fake pearl earring she'd lost. We were feeling our way through peanut shells and cigarette butts, searching for the clasp or the pearl, something to put back together. I remember, even in the dark, even when I couldn't see her features, I thought she was beautiful. I wanted to be like her.

"Are you sure you lost it here?" someone asked. "You sure you didn't lose it at home?"

There were only two other people in the place. The TV over the bar played game shows while sirens screamed outside. The bartender, a dreamy man who stared out the window as he smoked cigarettes, announced, "Hey, there's some commotion on your block," as nonchalantly as if he was commenting on the weather.

I recall how dizzy I felt when I stood up. We swallowed the rest of our wine and smiled. "Your teeth are purple!" Evelyn said, and we laughed. When we walked outside, I was blinded at first by the scorching sun.

It was Evelyn's house that burned down that afternoon while her baby was sleeping.

"Who would do something like that? Leave a baby alone?" the neighbors asked. I knew; I was standing right next to her while she cried and the police took her into custody. I stepped aside as they lead her away.

There was a judgment I made immediately which has stayed. The tightness of her sweaters, the shape of her face, her polished, press-on nails and fake jewels were despicable to me, and I felt disgust in my stomach for days. Since then, I have compared myself to her, and I'm not that bad.

Still at War

I put my hands up to my neck and tried to clear my throat. "Laryngitis," I whispered into the video camera. "I can't speak." The man from the church, a guy named Bruce Beck, was interviewing us—interviewing my husband. Bruce was from the Bentley Springs Baptist Church and wanted to put together a human-interest article for their monthly e-newsletter and website. Most of the time, he told us, he wrote short pieces about Bible Study or the Joy Club or "Getting Ready for the Real Jesus." But when he called to set up the interview, Bruce said he wanted to do a remembrance piece now that the war was nearly nine years old and almost over. "I don't want to intrude on your husband's privacy," he said. "But people need to know about our heroes. They want to feel supportive."

"You can ask," I told him, "but I don't know what kind of story you'll get. Douglas doesn't say much."

Bruce Beck was a clean-shaven church man in a pressed shirt who seemed genuine in his concern. He spent almost four hours listening to Douglas and watching *Apocalypse Now*. Douglas wouldn't shut up. I couldn't believe it. He said more than he had in the four months since he returned home. I eavesdropped from the kitchen, made bologna sandwiches and served drinks, but the voice I heard belonged to no one I knew, a stranger who spoke from my husband's body, referring to himself in a way I didn't recognize.

I had questions of my own. Before Douglas came home from Walter Reed, I went to the family advocacy briefing they gave for spouses and relatives. I raised my hand. But the advocacy woman droned on with her spiel about what we should expect our loved ones' state of mind to be when they came home. We were gathered in a cinderblock room in the hospital, a cold room with metal folding chairs and a podium at the front.

"Questions in a moment," the woman said and kept clicking through her PowerPoint presentation, something she had memorized, no doubt from countless times repeating it. I put my hand down. The woman next to me yawned and covered her mouth. She had round, thick wrists, with a child's hairband wrapped tight around the fat. A moment later, she nudged me with her elbow and pointed to a table on the other side of the room. There was a coffee urn and a tower of Styrofoam cups, a neatly displayed platter of flat, dry cookies. I wondered if the family services woman had gone to the trouble of arranging cookies in an elaborate effort to cheer us up. In the same cheery way, she was talking about our husbands, using terms that skirted around the fact that who we were getting back would probably not be the same men we'd been waiting for.

The speaker had an unfortunate haircut that made her look like Moe from the Three Stooges, a straight line of bangs that sliced across her forehead. As she talked, I tried to imagine a better hairstyle for her, something less severe. I was almost hoping Larry and Curly would burst into the room and interrupt the seriousness of what we were hearing. Instead, two psych nurses joined the presentation and passed out cards with a list of "Symptoms to Watch out For."

They said, "We understand your concern. We want to help if we can, but don't call us unless it's an emergency. Psychotic episodes are normal," they said. "They're not emergencies. Your husband might start drinking too much. Don't call us about that either. Don't call us unless he wakes you up in the middle of the night with his hands around your neck. Or with a knife at your throat. Or if you pass out. Something like that. That's when you should call. But don't call us unless that kind of thing happens. He'll have flashbacks, that's totally normal," they said.

"I can't listen to this," the woman next to me leaned in and whispered. "I want a cookie."

By the end of the presentation, my questions seemed irrelevant. I had wanted to know about depression if it came. I meant his, but in hindsight, I should've asked about my own.

"What has it been like to have your husband back?" Bruce asked me as I refreshed his iced tea. He was panning the video recorder toward me and probably had no idea how much effort I'd expended just to clean our apartment and make it seem normal. "I'm sure it's been quite a reunion!" he said.

I pointed at my throat. "Beyond words," I choked out hoarsely and I smiled. "I'm just happy he's here."

For the first few weeks after Douglas came home, I took time off from the custom upholstery shop where I'd gotten a job when I dropped out of college. I liked all the fabric patterns and colors; I liked recovering old pieces of furniture, and I was continually amazed how something torn and ratty could become a whole new furnishing with the right fabric. They were good to me at the shop, even made a cake with red and blue frosting when Douglas came home. In the beginning, every couple of days it seemed, I'd call work and tell them Douglas needed care. I was his sole caregiver. And they'd say, "OK, we understand." Then I'd lie down on the sofa and watch TV all day, talk shows and soap operas. We could barely afford cable.

Douglas was quiet, but he liked me to stay in the same room as him. He'd say, "I'm glad you're here. I'm glad to see you." He was like a chiming clock; he'd say it almost every hour in the break between TV shows. He'd grab my hand and stroke it for a moment, then just as quickly he'd forget I was there. He slept in the recliner most of the time, and occasionally would wake up in the middle of the night and hobble in to bed, throw his crutches on the floor, but he was still uncomfortable about letting me touch him. I watched him carefully, but the psych nurses had said not to ask. Douglas talked in his sleep, though, and in the beginning I listened. I could only imagine what he saw.

"Shut the fuck up, man!" he'd say to his friends. "How are you?" It was how they talked to each other on the phone whenever one of his war buddies called. They laughed in a way that was dark.

His emails to me when he was deployed had been different, more like the Douglas I wanted to know. He'd write, "Hi my love." He'd tell me about the children that followed them everywhere. On one trip across the expanse of desert, he told me how children showed up, from God knew where, in their bare feet, dust blowing all over them. They were looking for food and water. Douglas said he and the other guys kept driving, but they were silent, not knowing how to feel. "I want to feed them," he wrote. "But what do I have? Sticks of gum. It's like passing out Band-Aids and saying, 'I'm sorry.'"

One afternoon a week after he came home, Douglas started screaming in his sleep and thrashing in the recliner. I realized he was having a PTSD episode but my knowing it didn't stop it from happening. His arms cut through the air and he knocked the lamp off the table. It wasn't a great lamp, faux crystal that I got at the Goodwill, but it shattered. "Fuckin' towelhead!" he said. His words were unmistakable.

I bent down to pick up the broken shards of glass and I stared at him for a moment and saw someone I didn't like, a version of a man I might not have married. It was like suddenly realizing one day that you accidentally tied yourself to a stranger, maybe a tobacco-chewing hayseed who was as angry as he was skinny. What does that say about you? There were days I didn't want to be here, days I scolded myself for getting married too young, and other days I kicked myself for having these kinds of thoughts. I didn't tell anyone, certainly not my mother-in-law, who alternated between fits of crying and platitudes about how to "live and let live." It was her response to everything, as though the war would somehow stop if everyone just left everyone else alone. She'd gone off the deep end in some regards. "Don't worry. He will return to us," she told me on the phone one afternoon, as if, in fact, he had not already returned to us in this war-beaten package, one leg missing and a psyche that brewed storms.

I picked up those broken triangles of glass and tried to re-member what Douglas looked like when we first met. He had been almost like a Boy Scout, I thought. Exceedingly polite and clean cut. He worked as a driver for a delivery express service and occasionally went away on weekends to the Army National Guard. I liked that steadiness. It's what I needed. But something had changed after he got called up. Life had cut an extra line in his face; there was a thickness in his brow, in his being, his eyes deep with an expression I couldn't read. I threw the shards of glass away and let Douglas sleep. Then I sat on the sofa and watched TV because I didn't know what else to do. It was like I was wounded too, missing something I couldn't name.

When we met, I was still in community college studying drama, trying to keep up, believing that when I graduated I would go somewhere. I pictured myself moving to the city, hanging around artists and the theater and having fun. Douglas said he liked this about me, my dreams, and also the way I forced myself to be spontaneous even when I was tired. That's how we got married: in a flash. We had been dating five months and our time together had felt unreal. When Douglas got called up, I flew out to Fort Irwin, where he was getting weapon training and learning new strangleholds and personal combat stuff even though he was in a transportation unit. We got our blood tests and went to a justice of the peace and that was it. We were married two days before he left. I wasn't even wearing the dress I'd always dreamed of; instead, a pair of jeans and flip-flops. Douglas was in his fatigues and smelled of sweat. It was a scent I used to love.

A friend of Doug's, Bunnie (who was killed a few months later), snapped a picture of us outside the courthouse and that same day we had two copies made. We went to one of those thirty-minute photo joints and spent the first afternoon of our married life at the mall waiting for our wedding picture so each of us would have a copy. I remember being chilled from the mall air conditioning and Douglas pacing outside the Rite Aid. It was like waiting for a tiny birth, developing film, evidence to both of us that this had really happened.

When Douglas was deployed, I spent hours with our wedding picture, wishing it was somehow deeper than the thin sheet of waxy paper on which it was printed. I felt like I did when I was a kid and wanted to get inside the television to be with Dorothy in *The Wizard of Oz*, only this time I wanted to crawl inside that photo, reach through a hole to the other side of the world to get a hug and a dusty kiss and see what he was seeing. On those occasions when Douglas called from his company's cell phone, we'd get a couple of minutes with each other. Sometimes he'd talk in phrases I didn't understand but tried to memorize. He'd talk about IEDs and RPGs and patrolling the Celine Dion (Salah al-Din) mosque. It was all shorthand for war.

Douglas was speculating with Bruce about the money. The money he'd get from the government—that was his favorite topic. It was the only time he got excited, really animated and hopeful about the future. "What do you suppose they give for a leg? I know other guys who were in Walter Reed. They had missing fingers or half a liver gone or whatever, part of a stomach. What trumps a leg? Maybe blindness," he said. It was like a game of wounded poker, injured man against injured man. All the guys in Ward 57, the amputee ward, had talked this way. "I'd like to get a motorcycle," he told Bruce. "I've always wanted a Ducati."

Bruce looked at me.

I shrugged. "It seems kind of pointless," I whispered.

"No it doesn't!" Douglas said. "Not at all! It is not without its point."

Sometimes I wondered if Douglas was really aware that he couldn't yet stand up without hopping in place and holding his arms out straight to get his balance.

"I'll get a Ducati and then we'll buy a place of our own," he said. "And then we'll live off the rest."

"Really?" said Bruce. "How much do you expect to get?"

"We're still waiting to find out," I whispered. "I don't think it's much. The paperwork is tied up."

"It will be *plenty!*" Douglas insisted. "The Army doesn't leave behind its fallen."

"Right," I whispered. He didn't know. It was me, not Douglas, who had been on the phone with the Army benefits people for the last three weeks trying to convince them he deserved full disability. Full disability: that's what you wanted, that was the money hand in wounded poker. I coughed and tried to clear my throat. I looked over at Bruce, who was jotting something down.

I was embarrassed, afraid he would find out how we really lived. We were crowded in a small apartment with plain white walls that I tried to decorate with pictures I bought from a thrift store. They were pastels, the kind you see in doctors' offices. We had a ratty sofa that I covered with a sheet (I couldn't afford to reupholster my own furniture) and a powder-blue recliner for Doug. I'd draped the lampshades with scarves to hide the burn marks. Nothing matched but it was the best I could do, and I felt both proud of my efforts and ashamed. It was not what I wanted for my life.

I also didn't want Douglas to tell Bruce how we watched hour after hour of TV, how it carried us through the day. I didn't even read anymore. Instead, it was *Wheel of Fortune, Jeopardy,* and *Jerry Springer,* where at least all the freaks made us look normal for a while. There was a whole world full of crazies willing to parade on TV. It was reassuring that we were not alone, though I also felt embarrassed for us. Look what we had become: we ate Cheetos for breakfast, for Christ's sake. If Douglas wanted a Pepsi or a beer to wash them down at 9 a.m., I thought, Well, why not? He's injured. He deserves whatever he wants. The problem was the TV didn't stop. If it wasn't crappy game shows or soap operas, it was the news: the local and national broadcasts, even PBS. It was continual, always something else. But I couldn't turn it off because Douglas was tethered to it like it had become his prosthesis.

During commercial breaks, I tried to have conversations, but I didn't know what to say. "What was it like?" I asked once, but all Douglas told me was, "Believe me, you don't want to know." When I got home from work in the evenings I'd ask, "How are you feeling?" What I meant was, "Tell me anything, please."

Douglas would say, "I'm fine," or, "My leg hurts."

We answered questions, just not each other's. "What's an abolitionist?" I might answer Alex Trebek for a clue about twelve-letter words. Or Douglas would shout out, "The Crusades," before Vanna turned all the letters around, an answer I didn't suspect he even knew. Sometimes Douglas would ask, "Can you get me a beer, please?" but it wasn't a question of depth; it didn't mean anything beyond the fact that he was thirsty and felt helpless. I imagined maybe there was more behind it, things he'd never say: that he didn't want to seem like a burden, he didn't want to ask too much. How much is too much, I wonder? I didn't sign up for the Army, but look what I got.

I would never say this, though. I would never hold it against him. It's not his fault.

One evening on TV there was a commercial for a sports drink where a man in a wheelchair pushed himself around a racetrack, sweat pouring off his muscles. He was tanned and determined. The whole thing was meant to be inspiring but it seemed so unrealistic to me. What came before, I wanted to know. Did that guy in the wheelchair spend a year on the sofa, watching TV? I glanced over at Douglas, hoping he might get an idea, but he was asleep, reliving the war, or else dreaming about money the government was going to give him.

Bruce asked Douglas questions about desert geography while I stood quietly in the kitchen and stirred my iced tea. Bruce was one of those people who really supported the war, you could tell. I was relieved. I was afraid we had invited someone into the house who would ask questions like, did Douglas think it was worth it, his leg for oil, and so forth. They were too hard to think about, those things. Besides, if you're a family member, you've got to believe that what you're doing, giving up your loved one,

is the noble thing. It was what everyone told me. But sometimes an unrestrained thought would arise and I'd feel repulsed.
My stomach would turn, almost like morning sickness, and I'd
have to swallow the nausea. I could barely breathe. When these
moods hit, it helped to be at work. I'd rip the fabric off of old
chairs with my hands. I'd pull staples from the wooden frame
with a mind for tearing something apart. I was learning how to
sew kick pleats and tuck the extra fabric out of sight, but that's
all I knew how to do. It was frustrating. One afternoon, I messed
up several times on the same pleat and threw my plyers at the
wall. I didn't mean to, but I'd put a small dent in the plaster. I
spent the rest of the afternoon apologizing to my boss.

"Don't worry," he said like a command. He didn't say anything else. A couple days later, when I showed up for work, he
had an American flag thumbtacked to the wall in the workshop.
It covered the hole I'd made. My boss believed in the government the way some people believe in religion. It made it easier
on me. I was glad that Bruce believed, too, because if he had
questioned us too deeply, I don't know what I could've said.

In the other room I heard Bruce ask, "Would you go back again,
if you had the chance?"

"Hell, yeah! I'd go back in a second!" Douglas answered. He
was talking in the voice I couldn't stand. "It's not so bad. I don't
regret it one bit," he went on, like an endorsement for war.

Immediately, I felt my stomach drop. I knew it was hypo-
thetical, the possibility of him going back, but he didn't hes-
itate when he answered, not a millisecond of thought about
me and what I might want. What if I didn't want him to go?
What if I said no? I felt the nausea rise up again and tried to
swallow it. It was imaginary, this other life, but still it made
me sick.

Then Douglas called me into the living room. "Sweetie," he said. "Where's the movie?" It was his way of asking me to pop in the DVD for *Apocalypse Now*, which is what he watched nearly every day. By now, I'd seen it at least fifty times and I was over it. But Douglas would quote from it: "Charlie don't surf," or "You're in the asshole of the world, Captain." He had the whole thing memorized. For him, I guess, it was like stepping through, rejoining the action.

One afternoon when we'd returned from another doctor's appointment, the house was quiet, almost eerie without the sound of the television. Douglas hobbled toward his recliner, the uneven clop of his crutches on the wood floor. He said, "Every minute I stay in this room I get weaker." He startled me. I looked at him for a moment before I realized he was quoting.

"Are you serious?" I had asked. But he started laughing.

I found the DVD for Douglas and Bruce and slid it in the player. Then I stood up to leave. Douglas reached for me. "Watch it with us," he said. "I want you to be here."

I hesitated, then sat on the sofa. But I didn't pay attention. I stared at a picture on the wall that was crooked and considered getting up to straighten it.

"Imagine all this is sand," Douglas told Bruce about the jungle and the palm trees in the movie. "Imagine wearing flea collars around your ankles to keep all the fuckin' fleas from biting."

"No kidding," Bruce said.

"And then being loaded down with combat ammo: M16 ammo, grenades, smoke grenades, grenade-launcher ammo, and C-4."

"No kidding," Bruce said again. It was interesting to me how Bruce didn't talk about God that much. I thought that's all he would be saying.

They watched the movie for a half hour and no one spoke. It was almost like Bruce forgot why he was with us. The movie took over the room. Then Bruce asked, "After everything you've been through, if you had sons, would you encourage them to join the Army and fight?" He looked past Douglas when he spoke, not really listening for an answer. Perhaps he thought he already knew.

But Douglas said, "Fuck, no! Never!" He told Bruce, "I have a cousin who was going to sign up and I told him: forget it. Don't even think about it. No one should have to go through that shit."

I looked over at Douglas and wondered if he knew what he was saying. Just a moment ago he'd told Bruce he'd go back, no question. Was he being inconsistent? The fact that he'd absorb injury and risk his life but not want others to go through that—what else do you call that? It was not easy. There were so many days I wanted to trade and then there were moments like this.

Then Douglas turned back to the movie and it was gone. "Watch this part…this is the part where they play Wagner." He stopped the DVD and went back.

"Oh, right," Bruce said. "Wagner."

On the screen, the helicopters were coming in. Douglas and Bruce couldn't stop watching. It was the music. Douglas played it back again. He turned the volume all the way up. Bruce nodded. The music, the loudness filled everything. There was no room for me.

I felt sick and got up to leave.

"Wait." Douglas reached for my hand. I could barely hear him over the soundtrack, the strings and the horns and the copter blades. "Please," I thought I heard him say.

I didn't have it in me to say no. Anyway, who was I to deny him this much? I sat back down on the sofa. But I put my hands over my ears. "It's too much," I mouthed. "Turn it down."

Occasionally I thought about calling Moe, the advocacy woman, to ask if she had ever been married to a soldier who came back injured. I wanted to ask her: What do you do if they *don't* try to choke you? What if they suffocate you with silence instead? I wanted to know, what happens when you send a person away to war and that's it, they disappear? Then Bruce spoke. It was like he was reading my mind. He said, "What would you say to other Army families who have loved ones overseas?" On the TV, the fight scene was over but I didn't want to watch the rest of the movie. I knew what was coming.

"I'd tell them, I'm very proud of him," I whispered. Douglas smiled. I looked at him and smiled back. I coughed and tried to say it again, louder. If I had a voice, I'd tell them the war is not over.

The End of August

"Ah, when to the heart of man
Was it ever less than a treason
To go with the drift of things,
To yield with a grace to reason,
And bow and accept the end
Of a love or a season?"
—Robert Frost, "Reluctance"

We were alone together at the pool, swimming and resting in the sun. It was the slow end of August. The leaves were dark green, the sun running out. We hadn't seen each other for many months, though we had been in love once. That afternoon we were trying to be friends again somehow—perhaps in vain— and spend time together casually, as if the change between us had been slight, like a shadow lengthening.

The only other person at the pool was the lifeguard, who sat at a table under an umbrella and knew none of our history together. Perhaps to her we seemed married, like parents. She flipped through her magazine and bit her nails.

I cooled off in the water and swam laps. He slept in his lounge chair and gathered the last sunlight and warmth of the day. Shadows lengthened. I raced the light too, trying to swim as far as I could before the day faded. I was—I am—a strong swimmer, but I don't believe this has ever helped me in any significant way. I glided in the water, the length of the pool, arm over arm, back and forth, my body tracing the pattern of our relationship. At each turn I looked up from the water to see if he was watching. But he dozed, unaware of me except for the steady splashes I made. There was a measure to my breathing as I swam, a rhythm to his while he slept.

When I finished my laps, I lifted myself out of the pool and sat by the side for a moment, wondering at the quiet end of things, waiting for I'm not sure what.

The surface of the water was a mirror to the sun, the soft ripples gradually becoming flat and still. There was the silence of nothing, of birds flitting overhead and car doors closing, of lawnmowers in the distance. I stood and patted myself dry and dripped on the cement near my chair. The droplets seeped into the cement and formed strange shapes as they merged together. Shapes that would eventually dry and disappear.

His eyes were closed but he knew where I stood, had always stood. He roused himself barely and said something.

"How was it?" he asked. We hadn't spoken much lately.

"This is my favorite time of day," I said. I was trying to say exactly what I meant.

The sun sank slowly into early evening. I didn't want to let go yet. It's difficult for me to leave a place by the water in late August. Just one more minute, I think every day, every year. Just a little bit more. I wanted to gather the sun to my chest, hold it, keep it still and alive. I was usually alone this time of day but I didn't want to tell him that.

I said, "I wonder how far I swam. How long is this pool, do you think? How many feet?"

"I don't know," he said, "a hundred?"

"No, not a hundred," I replied, answering my own question. "Maybe seventy-five."

"Maybe."

I liked having his company even if there was nothing left between us. We were comfortable by the water, but not in love. Whatever was said now held no meaning.

He stretched in his chair, then stood up. He walked away from me. He leaned over the edge of the pool as if he were examining the filters. Then he jumped in. He splashed a bit and swam on his back, his ears underwater, his face toward the sky. He floated and kicked and pulled himself across the pool. He doesn't swim as well as I do, but that has also never mattered.

The lifeguard flipped through her magazine. The trees swayed with a breeze. The sun had moved and I was in a shadow, alone. I was usually alone. I watched him swim and pretended to read my book. For a while I wished for something else.

I Get There Late

I get there late, 10:30 at night, and they're slow about opening the door. They're not expecting me, and I'm guessing Jack's wife—a bland woman, formerly a friend of mine—is already in bed. The dog barks as soon as I pull in the driveway. I hear the baby cry. The porch light flicks on as I pull my luggage from the trunk. I'll tell you this: I take my time.

Jack's at the screen door and his wife is next to him in her bathrobe, holding the baby. The porch light shines in their eyes, making it impossible for them to see me; I'm a shadow. "Who's there?" they say, as though I'm a burglar creeping around their house. They shield their eyes, searching the distance, a big dark void, to find me.

This is how I do it: I march up the sidewalk lugging my suitcase next to me and I say, "Surprise" without enthusiasm, as if they should've known I'd show up, after all these years. There's a hint of challenge in my voice.

"Oh my God!" Jack says, not unfriendly. "What are you doing here?"

"Jesus," my former friend says. She tries to sound excited, but her voice is like mine and betrays her. She's rattled and cautious, like she's just spotted a spider inching toward her bare feet. She can't hide her apprehension, her reluctance to invite me in. We stand for a few minutes, exchanging pleasantries, me with my suitcase tugging on my arm and my friend closing her robe tighter at her neck and scooching the baby farther up her hip.

"It's been ages!" Jack says. "What have you been up to?"

"Oh, you wouldn't believe it! *Sooo much* has happened!" I exaggerate. "For starters, I quit my job today." They try not to blink or seem like they're judging me. "Then I just started driving. I'm on my way to Florida for vacation," I lie. I tell them I thought of them at the last minute.

We talk politely, but they still don't invite me inside. I tell them half-truths, and they nod. We act like we're not uncomfortable with each other. The wife, she jogs the baby to her other hip. She listens to me as if I were a traveling salesman or a Jehovah's Witness trying to sell her something she doesn't quite want. She would just as soon close the door without remorse.

"Listen," I finally say, "I want to apologize for everything back then. I've really changed a lot in the last few years." I don't mean it, but I say it because I want them to let me in. I have nowhere else to go. The dog is looking at me through the screen door. He wags his tail.

"Oh," Jack says. "Don't worry about it." I have no idea how much he remembers, but he pretends he knows what I'm talking about. He pretends it's water under the bridge. The wife, she half smiles, though she's suspicious. She's still not a believer, no matter what good news I or the Jehovah's Witnesses have to share.

"How about a drink?" Jack says. "You thirsty?" He opens the screen door. I don't say yes or no, but I pick up my suitcase and step inside. I find a chair in the living room and sink into it, then park my purse and suitcase on the floor next to me and look around.

This is not how I pictured it. Not them, not their house. Their furniture is so heavy and immovable you could sink a ship with it. There are toys and shoes and clothes strewn about; a tent set up in the living room, filled with stuffed animals for the baby; a chalkboard in front of the fireplace blocking the hearth; newspapers scattered across the floor in a lazy attempt to housetrain the dog. There are pee stains. An antique coffee table is stacked with dirty dishes. I can barely take it all in. I had not expected to dislike their lifestyle. From the outside of this house, I had expected to be envious. I'd planned on hating these people and disrupting their life. They have two boats in the driveway.

"God, I feel terrible—I got here so late and woke the baby," I say. "I should've called first. Maybe I shouldn't have come." I prop my feet up on the ottoman and relax.

"Forget it!" Jack says, fixing drinks in the kitchen. I'm guessing he's had a few already, based on his levity, his willingness to forget. "What's your poison?" he calls to me.

"Nothing," I say, and this is true. I don't drink anymore, but they don't know that.

"*What?*" he yells from the kitchen, meaning he's heard something unbelievable.

"Nothing," I answer. "Water's fine."

"I don't want anything either," the wife calls out, though no one has asked her. She warms to me just slightly. The baby fusses on her lap. "You're not drinking," she says in a whisper. "You always drink."

"Yeah, well, I stopped for a while."

"Tell that to Jack," she mutters. She's sick of it, I can tell—plus she was always a lightweight, unable to keep up—and for a split second I almost feel sympathy for her. We're silent for a moment, even the baby and the dog and the television. Then I pat her hand and smile as though I want things to work well for her. She doesn't move. We both know I'm not here as a long-lost friend, a miracle of compassion showing up on her porch just in time to throw their marriage a buoy. I'm here to get away from *my own* mess, not straighten out theirs. You'd think with two boats and a BMW they could hire a maid. It's lakefront property, for God's sake. Meanwhile, I'm broke and middle-aged, an underemployed secretary who was recently fired.

Hey, but who cares? It's not like they've been wondering about me these last few years. Not since Jack's wife got pregnant, ensuring their marriage. It was a hysterical pregnancy, not even the real thing, so I can't say I'm indulgent of their giant mess or the fact that Jack's wife wants him to stop drinking. Let's just say, if I were bent on revenge—and I'm not—there'd be very little left to destroy.

"So!" Jack says, entering the living room with three glasses, two waters and a whiskey. "So…here you go." He hands a glass to me and another to his wife. He raises his glass and cheers.

"So…yeah!" I answer, as if I know what I want to say next.

We're quiet again. The wife shifts in her seat.

"So, what kind of mileage did you get?" Jack finally asks.

"I made pretty good time," I say, "considering."

I tell Jack about my route here, and he listens. I try to catch his eye to stir what I'm saying into something more than what I'm saying. His wife is yawning and trying to smile. She encourages the baby to crawl from her lap and toddle toward me. The baby grabs my purse next to the chair, then pulls herself and my purse onto my lap. We laugh. This is supposed to be endearing. I try to hide the edge in my voice, the inflection that says, "Please keep your child away from me." I talk to the baby as though she's an adult while she plays with my car keys. "Sure, you can borrow my car," I say. "Just make sure you fill up the tank." The baby squirms on my lap. She digs deeper into my purse and pulls out lipstick.

"Honey, you don't need that yet," I say. "That's for years later, when you're still trying to trap a husband, like I am." I make a joke to get them to laugh. Instead, the wife turns to Jack and rubs his arm. This is her insult to me, though

I'm trying to pretend bygones are bygones. I'm going out of my way to make these people feel comfortable. I tell them I admire their taste in furniture. "Everything is so solid," I say, and they agree. They tell the story about how their dining room table was refinished.

The baby draws lipstick on her face and squeals. Then she aims the lipstick for my nose. I try to stop her, but she smudges a line across my cheek, then squirms from my lap. Jack's wife doesn't say anything. She hands me a tissue and smiles as if she has somehow orchestrated this slight. The wife is overweight and tired. She sits on the sofa like a permanent object. She has an old robe tied around her waist, and she yawns while the baby scoots around the room with my lipstick. I chase the child to grab it back and to prevent her from creating more of a mess, not that they would notice. This is so unlike me, I think, to chase a baby. Next to Jack and his wife, I seem almost responsible, even if I did steal the lipstick and a few other things from a convenience store on my way here. The baby pulls me by the hand to the chalkboard. Jack and his wife are entertained. I perform with their child while they tell me about the veneer on their furniture. We talk in fits and starts; I make cooing sounds and say things like, "Oh my goodness, what a good artist you are!" while the baby makes indiscriminate lines on the board. They tell me the name of the furniture company, a father and son team. "No, no, no, not on the fireplace," I say. I draw pathetic circles and stems on the chalkboard, stick-figured flowers to keep the baby's attention. They explain how difficult it was to move the table back into the dining room without scratching it.

"We covered it in blankets. It took us two hours!" they say.

Let me tell you: I don't give a shit. This is not why I came. I'm not interested in the married side of being married.

The wife offers to show me the house, to display the wardrobe and nightstand which were also refinished. Our exchange is stilted as I follow her from Jack's den to their bedroom to the baby's room. We pad across the carpet in our bare feet. She lingers in their bedroom to show me the bedframe, as if to prove a point.

When we get to the baby's room, she says, "This is where you'll be staying." The dog follows us, his nails clicking on the hardwood floor. "You'll have to lock the door," she says. "The baby and the dog will want to come in around 6 a.m. They might scratch at the door."

"That's OK," I say, even though I'm already annoyed. "Oh, look!" I cheer. "This room is *darling*. I love the ducks painted on the walls."

"The baby loves water," the wife says, momentarily dropping her guard. "She loves to take baths."

This is boring to me, but I smile. I say, "I noticed you've got a sailboat in the driveway."

"Oh, God," the wife whispers. "Don't mention it to Jack. It puts him in a bad mood. Every time he tries to sail, it's a disaster."

When we get back to the living room, Jack is pouring himself more whiskey. He's abandoned the pretense of going to the kitchen for ice and has brought the bottle with him to the coffee table. The TV is flickering with the sound turned down, and the baby is digging through my purse again. It's a regular Norman Rockwell scene.

Then the baby sees Jack's glass and goes for the whiskey. "Mine," she says. Jack gives her a sip. She makes a sour face, but two seconds later wants another sip. Jack tilts his glass for her again.

"Don't do that," the wife says. "Why do you do that?"

"She wanted it," Jack says, as if he had no choice. The baby makes a noise and moves toward the glass.

"No," the wife says, and she turns the baby and points her in my direction. The baby wiggles toward me and pulls a pen from my purse. She aims it at my luggage and begins to scribble.

"No!" I say, and pry the pen from her hand. I unwrap her tiny fingers while trying not to upset her. Neither Jack nor his wife bother to discipline the child. They seem to enjoy watching me grapple with their toddler. "Not that, either," I say, snatching my lighter from her. The baby starts to cry. "Lighters are not for little girls who might burn themselves!"

The baby screams. The pitch hurts my ears. I knew I shouldn't have come. What was I expecting? The baby's face is red as she shrieks in undulating waves. I can smell the whiskey on her tiny breath.

Finally, Jack's wife pushes herself off the sofa, comes over to me, and lifts the baby from my lap.

"Enough," she says. "Somebody's tired." She means herself *and* the baby; she means I woke them up. "There are sheets on the bed in the baby's room," she says to me. "The baby will sleep with us." She shoots Jack a look. She does not say, "You come to bed soon, too," but she means it. She means, "Don't drink so much," and she means, "Don't stay up late with this woman." A warning. Then she disappears into the bedroom and shuts the door.

Jack lights a cigarette and fixes himself another drink. "You sure you don't want one?"

I do, but I say, "No thanks." Why do I want things I don't even want? For a second, there's a renewed ease between us, an intimacy in our exchange, as though time and our emotions have not passed. I'm moved by the tenderness in Jack's voice. I imagine every night might be this way if we were married. But I remind myself it means nothing: he offered me a drink and I didn't take it. That's all. It seems profound, though. I used to feel like I should say yes to anything Jack offered me, ever.

"Hey, I changed my mind—I'll take a refresher. A few more ice cubes for my water." This is as much as I will permit myself. Jack gets up and takes my glass into the kitchen, and I can hear the icemaker on the refrigerator door splash cubes into my glass. I look at the picture frames on the end table—snapshots of the baby, one of Jack and the baby asleep on the sofa.

"Have you seen anyone from the old days?" he asks when he comes back into the room. We went to high school together twenty years ago—Jack and I—and it seemed like a separate lifetime ago, its own marriage of sorts.

"Anyone from the old days," I muse. He thinks he's asking a safe question, that by talking about other people we will avoid talking about ourselves. Maybe he knows why I'm here and he's trying to sidestep the emotional quicksand, but I want to talk about it, push him into the pit and make the conversation uncomfortable. I watch him gulp his whiskey and wonder what Jack recalls, if he remembers our attraction, our unspoken relationship while he was dating the woman who is now his wife.

"Hank got married," I say, pretending to go along with him. I move forward in my chair and stretch my leg so my foot is nearly touching his. "He married a twenty-two-year-old dancer he met in a whirlwind. And Tom T. moved to Las Vegas with Jerry, still trying to get rich quick," I laugh. I rattle off old names of people we vaguely remember, who are like cartoon characters to us now. I touch Jack's bare foot with mine. I keep it there.

"And I heard that guy, Hugh Poe, died," I say as an afterthought. "You know Sue moved to Texas?"

"Yeah, I heard about Sue," he says. "How'd Hugh Poe die?"

"I dunno," I tell him, "I just heard he died." I shift my skirt and cross my legs so my calf muscle is emphasized and my legs look long and shapely. "Stacy got remarried and had her fifth baby. Five seems like an ungodly number, doesn't it?"

"I always liked Hugh Poe," Jack says, in a detached sort of way. He downs his whiskey and is quiet as he pours himself another. He moves his foot away from mine, gets up, and grabs a pack of cigarettes from the mantel. When he sits back down, he almost steps on my toes.

"I always liked Hugh Poe," he says again.

"I don't really remember him," I say. "He wasn't anyone I'd really remember."

"He...was..."Jack says, "quiet and slow....A really...good-natured guy." Jack's words are deliberate and somewhat slurry. He lights his cigarette, then exhales. "I wonder how he died."

I indulge Jack's melancholy, though I couldn't care less. I sigh. "I knew he was slow," I say. "I thought he was just dimwitted or something."

"He was simple," Jack says meditatively. "Like something was wrong with him." Jack's eyes are heavy, as if the grief, not the whiskey, is weighing on him. We're silent together, but the old intensity between us, the quiet attraction that used to turn our silences into a sort of passion, has faded. The conversation is flat.

"He wasn't quite right," Jack repeats. He draws on his cigarette.

After a time, I say, "Hey, I have an idea! I know what we can do!"

(For the record, let me just say: I'm here to enjoy myself, have a vacation. That's the only reason I mention it.)

"Here's my idea," I say. "How about if you take me sailing on your boat tomorrow? Your wife says she doesn't sail with you, but I'll go! We'll have a great time. Or we could go now and sit on the dock. What do you think?"

Jack is silent a moment, staring at his hands, trying to focus. "How'd he die again?" he asks.

I stare at him a moment to see if he's serious. "Maybe he fell overboard and drowned," I say. "No one knows."

"He drowned?"

Jack's stuck on the same note. Getting his attention, at this point, seems meaningless. But I lean forward and stretch. I put my hand on his thigh and squeeze. "You know Davey Miller got divorced again?" I say. "I heard he bought his wife a fur coat, but she wore it naked to her lover's apartment and Davey chased her down to get it back." I laugh and play with my hair. "Have you heard from him?" My hand is still touching Jack, but I'm leaning at an odd angle, so I slide my hand across his leg as I sit up. He knows what I mean.

Jack is quiet as he draws on his cigarette. "I don't know," he says. "It always seems pointless." He's not ignoring me, I'm sure. But I give up and roll my eyes—not at his drunkenness, which is the same, but at his gloom. I find it hard to believe that he is genuinely upset by Hugh Poe's death, as though many years ago some small piece of Jack was altered, was pulled in another direction by knowing Hugh. Grief is a wreck: the relationships of things to each other forever shifting and colliding. I imagine the real source of Jack's grief is that he's sick of being married to *her*. But he doesn't say that.

Jack stamps out his cigarette and lights another. He stares into the ashtray that's full of butts crimped in the shape of commas, each cigarette the punctuation between thoughts, an ashtray full of meaningless moments. This is all inconsistent with the way things used to be.

"Well," I say as consolation, "he died a while ago. Anyway, it's hard to fuck up your life when you're that slow; you don't make such a mess." For a split second, I almost mean what I say. I almost wish I'd known Hugh Poe enough to comprehend his simplicity. It might've helped me.

"How'd he die?" Jack asks again.

"I don't know," I say. "Why was he slow?"

"I don't know," he answers.

And that's it. Jack is drunk. His eyes are red and sag. It's too much work to sway him this evening, to flirt and get him interested in me. He's caught in a swirl of melancholy, and I'm bored. I have nothing in common with him anymore.

"Hey," I say, "it's late. I'm going to bed," but I don't move, waiting for him to want me to stay. Waiting for something to be different.

He mutters something and shakes his head. He can barely put a thought together. And still, I find him attractive, just like the old days, except he's put on a few more pounds and has grown a small bump on the side of his cheek. I'm not sure I would love these things about him if we had been the ones who'd gotten married, but I find him appealing, the idea of him is appealing. Or maybe I just want to wreck something.

"See you in the morning," I say, finally. I get up and drag my suitcase down the hall to the baby's bedroom. "Goodnight," I say one more time and close the door.

The baby's room is cheerful and dreamy, with smiling fish painted around the walls, ducks floating above them on water. Tiny stars are stuck to the ceiling. I strip out of my clothes and crawl under the comforter, sink into the overstuffed pillows on the double bed. I stretch out and look around me: I'm young and delighted for a few moments. Nearly winning. Jack is in the other room, I can almost feel it. Above me is the glow of stars. When I turn, I see a clown lamp laughing silently on the nightstand. I have the urge to smash it.

Things might've been different. If I were simple like Hugh Poe, none of this would bother me. I stare at the constellations above me and have a sudden notion to stand on the bed and pick those stars off the ceiling, see if anyone would notice. I crawl out of the covers and bounce a little on the mattress. Then I stretch up and rearrange stars. How often do they look at the ceiling, anyhow? Perhaps one day it'll strike them that certain things have been lost or altered, but they won't know exactly how it happened, and they won't remember how to put it back the way it was. I smile at myself in the baby mirror. Ha, my joke on them.

Fixed

"Went to the party very discouraged
I watched the litter pile like a wall
I looked at the river, just couldn't forgive it
It was ladened with all kinds of shit."
—Patti Smith, "Don't Say Nothing"

What else looks like that? Floating and caught, head down like it's watching the bottom of the river, it reminds me of something. I follow the balloon of the body as it bobs in the water, but I don't tell anyone.

Everyone is dancing. I stand in the corner, staring out the window at the river below. I'm in a shadow of the warehouse loft, wondering why I expected to have fun at this godforsaken party. It's Oliver's crowd; I knew this before I came, but I thought it would be different. People are talking behind me in the background. They're laughing. The warehouse is dark with colored lights and smells like dust and metal. A welder lives one floor below, and his sculptures have been hauled up the freight elevator for this art show. He builds life-size monsters made from scrap metal and trash. They appear stunned, like walking dumpsters surprised to find themselves in this state—not altogether different from the people at this party. I'm surrounded by freaks: unstable artists and bohemian slackers, some of whom I recognize. I lean against the wall and watch them. From my corner, I imagine I'm hovering above them, seeing them without being seen, being here without belonging, condemned to this point of view.

I came here for the drummer, some guy I met in a coffee shop who had tattooed sleeves and Asian symbols inked around his neck. He invited me to come to the warehouse where his band, Lisa from Tokyo, would be playing. He handed me a flyer—he'd handed everyone a flyer—but he smiled at me and said, "Hope you can make it," and I believed him, I believed he meant, "Hope *you* can make it," as in, me. I was flattered. Not many guys are bold enough to approach me. I'm a depressive type in combat boots, tall and scrawny with bony shoulders and uncombed hair that falls in my eyes. I am not what you would call beautiful, though my appearance isn't an accident. I want to look this way.

"OK," I said, staring at the flyer in my hand.

"I'll look for you." He winked. I nodded. I didn't know what else to say.

Later, I realized I could've introduced myself—"I'm Jane"— or asked him what kind of music he played. But I didn't think of it on the spot, so I came to the party to meet him again, have a conversation.

From my perch as overseer, I watch the drummer in the opposite corner. He keeps up a hypnotic beat behind a song the bass player is obviously improvising. The room is smoky, the music slow and ghostly. Suddenly the guitar screeches loud and monstrous, then low again. The singer is so fucked up he's hanging onto the mike stand for support. He moans to the music as if he's wounded. The drummer can't see me; he barely has his eyes open, nodding to the beat of the song. I like watching him, though. He's attractive to me and seems familiar, tough and helpless, sad but trying not to show it. A lost boy who flirts with excess and escape. He reminds me of someone who will die tragically and stupidly. For that reason, he reminds me of Oliver. A waste. Another dead artist.

Oliver was a filmmaker, and he'd filmed a series of beautiful shorts I loved. Oliver shot my favorite film in the winter, in the city, when the streets were shut down. There was a single man in the frame, walking away from the camera, huddled against a snowstorm. Oliver put an original score to the film. That's all it was: the lonely sound of a piano and a man walking in the snow.

I often wish I could see that film again, but his family has it now. They collected his things from our apartment after he died. I think they blame me, as if I were the cause of death. I know he was going to ask me to marry him. He said he fell in love with me the first night we met, but that was because we were both drunk. We lived together for a year, and if he were alive, I'm sure we would be laughing right now. He said I was the funniest person he knew, and he appreciated my jokes, my warped view of the world. He thought I was smart. He turned twenty-eight right after he OD'd, almost five months ago.

I stare at the drummer, at his tattoos and muscular forearms and wish him better luck. If I had the nerve to approach him, I'd say, "Good luck." Or even, "Be careful," though I never said any of this to Oliver. I admit I never said stop.

"What are you talking about?" the drummer would probably answer. "Are you a friend of Sherri's?"

Sherri is a person around whom circles develop, a hairdresser who studies fashion, and for that reason people hang on her every word.

"That's really deep," she says. "Like panic." She is sitting in a pit of sofas near me, smoking weed and attempting to talk about art. She's wearing a pink wig and leather turquoise platforms, hot pants and a sheer black top. No bra, of course, and that's what everyone is listening to. They're paying rapt attention.

"It looks like water," she says. "Like drowning in water. See the mouth and the bubbles? Just imagine!"

"That's cool," some guy says, as though drowning is cool, is something he's lived through and is willing to try again.

Next to him sits a fifty-year-old junky bisexual with dreads whom everyone loves, literally. She puts her head on the drowning guy's shoulder.

"What made you paint it?" she asks the artist.

The artist is wearing an undersized sports coat and a crushed fedora. He tells the crowd gathered around him how Rilke was influential to the process of painting, how love and solitude entered into it. "Love is such a lonely road," he says and looks away.

I snort at this but he can't hear me. *What a fake. It's evident from your painting that you don't know crap!* I almost yell. No one is standing around me or looks in my direction. No one sees it as I do.

"Rilke," they say. "How interesting."

"He's the shit," the artist says.

I turn away from them and peer out the window again. I can't believe all the trash floating by. There is an empty warehouse on the other side of the falls. Stinkweeds grow on both sides. The stream pours down the middle, carrying sticks and bottles and bits of paper. I've lost sight of the thing that was bobbing in the water. Perhaps it's moved on; perhaps it was saved.

Occasionally, people walk toward me and say hi as they grab a few pretzels from a bowl. They don't stay long. It's like I have a circle of ill will around me, the way I stand with my arms crossed, pushing everyone away with my thoughts. "Don't talk to me," I nearly say. "Don't ask." Too much silence, though, can kindle an implosion, create a big mess on the inside. Other times I'm afraid I'll open my mouth and words will erupt everywhere, a disaster of words I have not given permission to bound out of my mouth.

"Hey, Jane," a girl says.

"Hey," I answer.

I know these people through Oliver, though not very well. I know them by sight and gossip. I know a few of them from the funeral. They said, "Man, I'm *really* sorry," and shook my hand in the reception line, but they don't know me, just that I am the girlfriend Oliver left behind. I'm like a ghost to them, an idea of a person. Most people know enough to leave me alone. They know I read a lot of books and don't talk much. Even dead, Oliver is more real to them than I am. But that's OK. Anonymity has its vantage point, its perks.

For instance, they don't know—thank God—that my mother hustled me off to born-again boot camp two weeks after Oliver died. She said it would make me feel better to be surrounded by people my own age. She was trying to reform me, put me in touch with Jesus so I could be saved—not only from grief, but from the useless life of a nonbeliever. I went because I didn't say no.

The cure didn't take, of course. I was surrounded by a slew of smiling twenty-somethings; I felt older, weighed down, too old for all the hopeful god shit. So I refused to hold hands and sing along with the guitar or get excited about the end of the world Jesus had coming.

Secretly I felt peace at the camp, though I would never admit it. I enjoyed sitting on the shore of the lake and throwing stones into the water. I liked the sound of the rocks sinking. I found a fossil with a partial imprint of a leaf. I turned it over in my hands unconsciously for hours like a worry bead and carried it everywhere. By the end of the week, the only thing I fully understood about myself, drilled into me by smiling Southern Baptists, was that I didn't have faith, and this would be my downfall.

"Do you believe your savior Jesus Christ loves you?" they asked one afternoon. There were two of them, a blond girl and her smiley-face boyfriend.

I didn't want to answer them. If I believed in something, I didn't know what to call it. Even if there were a God, I would not have admitted it. "I believe in this fossil," I said. "This fossil rules."

"You'll need more than that," the girl said, exasperated.

"I think life should be made like this fossil," I said. "Stable, permanent; if there *is* a God, I think he messed up in the design."

"God can be your fossil," the clean-cut boyfriend said. "He can stay fixed in your life like that."

"Oh, *please*," I snorted. "Do you people ever give up? What if I said God should be a hula dancer, what would you say then? That God works through grass skirts?" I turned my head away to look out toward the water.

"That's fear," the guy said.

"No, that's funny," I answered. "If you think about it, grass skirts *do* have a certain power to sway men." I wouldn't look at them.

"Let's go," the girl whispered. "It's obvious she's hopeless."

Hopeless/godless—the girl said it as if the words were interchangeable. She moved away quickly; I think she was afraid my doubts were contagious. I've learned people don't like to be around grief.

Another girl I know walks by me at the party and smiles with pity-eyes. She keeps her distance but regards me as if she knows what I must be going through, as if she understands. She'd had a crush on Oliver at some point—they shot up together—but as far as I'm concerned, she's a proprietress of nothing.

On the last day of camp, I'd seen a black snake stretched out on a rock near the parking lot. He was long and curved like a shredded old tire, perfectly still, warming himself in the sun. I liked him. A couple of people were standing around the snake, waiting for it to move. Then a counselor came up to look at it. He had a shovel with him, and I expected him to scoop up the snake, to push it away so no one would get hurt. But he lifted the shovel above the rock and came down hard, chopping the snake in half.

"It's not poisonous!" I said, louder than I expected. The counselor looked up at me for an instant, then went back to the task of pounding the snake's head and shoveling the two halves off to the side. Some guys laughed. I was dumbfounded. For a split second I saw myself as someone else. I saw myself grab the shovel from the clean-shaven church man and pound him over the head with it. I howled as this other version of myself, swinging the shovel like a bat, and took out a row of them. I was unstoppable.

"Who do you think you are?" I said. "You're not God; you don't have a right to kill that snake!" What I meant was: this kind of death was empty and wasteful, life chopped in half unnecessarily. I should've seen it coming. But I didn't stop the man, and I blamed myself for that, as if, by speaking sooner, I might've prevented something. Even with Oliver, there were words I kept to myself, words I realize now could've saved at least one of us.

I tried to tell my mother about the snake on the way home.

"I'm sure the man was just doing his job," she said.

"Fuck you," I muttered. She started weeping then, and we didn't say anything for the rest of the ride.

For a few weeks after that I stayed in the apartment. I watched black-and-white movies in the dark and listened to angry rock music with divas screaming. I ate cereal for dinner and lost weight. There was something beyond grief I couldn't find. "Shouldn't she be over him by now?" Oliver's friends were probably asking each other, but they didn't say as much to me.

Maybe they were right. If it had been me who died, I suspect Oliver wouldn't have come to a halt as I have. First, he'd get high and pretend he was fine. He knew so many people from his prep-school days and from college before he dropped out, then film people and artists. He wouldn't be alone like I am. If he were here, he'd be in the epicenter of the party. I know this, but I cannot imitate what he would do, I cannot be him. Instead,

I stand by myself between the tall warehouse windows. I move occasionally, from window to window, and pretend I'm supposed to be here.

The band finishes playing their song and the musicians take a break and disappear into a back room. Everyone else scatters throughout the warehouse. A few people come over to the windows to cool off in the breeze. They hang out in the makeshift kitchen and grab beers out of the cooler. I scoot over so I'm next to the counter. A guy comes toward me carrying a bag of ice. In the dark he looks like someone I know.

"Hey, Patti Smith!" he calls. He's talking to me, to my ratty hair and wrinkled state. "Can you hold this?" He dumps the ice into my arms. He tilts his straw cowboy hat at me. I realize he is not the person I thought he was, but he talks with me as if we're friends.

He leans over and opens the cooler next to me. There is a paperback in his pocket; I imagine it's a book about spirits and poetry, but I can't make out the title. The cowboy is thin and strong, with long sideburns, good-looking in a well-read kind of way. His shirt is unbuttoned, and he has a smooth chest. I immediately like him, though I don't trust him. He seems like the kind of guy who attracts beautiful, fucked-up girlfriends.

"OK," he says. "Dump it here." I tear the plastic bag and let the ice cubes fall into the cooler. "I'm making margaritas," he says. "You know anything about it?"

"Why are you asking me?" I accuse, as if there is a crime in it.

"God. Are you part of this party? Help me out," he says. Then, "Here, hold this."

He hands me a box and pulls a mixer out of the cabinet. In the process, he knocks over a bag of cat food sitting on the counter. Food pellets scatter everywhere.

"You know, you're not a very good flirt," he says. "The gruff approach doesn't become you."

"You dropped something," I say, and point to the pellets of cat food.

"Yeah, yeah, yeah," he answers, which means he's not going to sweep it up.

"What happened to the cat?" I ask. This is as close as I get to telling anyone what I saw in the river.

"What are you talking about?"

He takes the box from me and shoves it back inside the cabinet. There's a mirror inside the door, and he checks himself out. Then he pulls me next to him so we're looking at each other.

"'Sometimes it is necessary to reteach a thing its loveliness,'" he says. He winks at himself in his cowboy hat. I roll my eyes and step aside.

"Did you just make that up?" I ask.

"I'm quoting," he says.

"Who?"

"No idea," he says, "but you could use a page from that book." I can't tell if he's joking or being kind, whether he likes me or feels sorry for me.

"You don't even know what book," I say.

"There you go again," he says. "Pouring on the charm."

"I used to be funny," I inform him.

"Yeah, I can tell." When he bends down to plug the mixer into an outlet, I see his book again, sticking out of his pocket. I want it to be profound, a book that I recognize, one that would make me like him. We could have a conversation about it. But I have a hard time reading the title upside down; the letters look like they should spell "Flaubert," but I can't make it out completely.

"Hey, what's your book?" I ask.

"I don't know," he says. "Someone just gave it to me." He empties a bottle of tequila into the mixer. "Something about outer space." My heart sinks. I was hoping for a sign, an answer to something.

The cowboy presses a button on the blender. He leans close to me and says something in my ear, but I can't hear it for the whirring of the blades.

"What?" I ask. I nearly shout.

He just smiles as if I heard him, as if I'm in disbelief. He turns the blender off and winks.

Sherri in her pink wig comes up behind him then, presses herself against his back. "Can I have a little drinky-winky?" she asks. She is taller than him in her turquoise platforms.

"Test it for me," he says. "How is it?"

"Baby," she answers, "I don't care."

Before I can say anything more to the cowboy, a crowd of people line up for margaritas. They reach around me to grab cups.

"You'd better get some before it's all gone," the cowboy says.

"That's OK," I answer.

I stroll across the room toward the back door, where the musicians have disappeared. I pass paintings on the wall, most of them abstract and meaningless. There are canvases speckled with paint that seem exhausted with too many layers.

On another wall, there's a large shadowbox full of photographs and voodoo dolls. A second box is filled with clay figures, people caught in mid-action behind glass. The figures are pinned to velvet, arranged like a Victorian butterfly collection. I notice a woman figurine that's asleep with her mouth open; there's a mirror glued to the outside of the box where, theoretically, the viewers are supposed to see themselves and understand the connection, as if we're all asleep with our mouths open, or pinned to a wall, caught in a box, something obvious like that.

Farther down the wall, I find a series of nude drawings I like. They seem so simple and light in comparison, single lines defining a body without the mess of splattered paint. There is a drawing of a pregnant nude and that holds my attention: the roundness of possibility, the big balloon of hope. I turn away quickly, afraid of my own blank space.

I walk toward the back door. Next to the door stands a metal sculpture of a man named "Who?" made of found objects. He wears a trashcan lid as a hat. His face is a series of oily bicycle gears, and he appears startled, his mouth an O. His arms are folded across his chest, and he has a circle of syringes welded to his heart. "Hey, Oliver," I say to the garbage head. "Glad you could make it."

I've heard our relationships with the dead continue long after the bodies are gone. Perhaps they're the most profound relationships we have, those big conversations with nothing. Lately I've been wishing for this relationship with Oliver to be over, for him to die completely. Meanwhile, I run into him in the stupidest places, him looking more and more surprised to be dead. "Oh!" he seems to say. "How did I get *here*? How could *this* have happened?" I get angry with him then, when the answer is obvious.

The door to the back room opens a sliver and someone I don't know squeezes out into the gallery. He's careful not to let anyone else into the room.

"Hey," I say, "is the drummer back there?"

"Who?"

"The drummer?"

The guy just shrugs and walks away. Then the door opens again, and this time it's the drummer who comes out. "Hi! Remember me?" I almost say. But the drummer wanders past, and I let him go. I recognize the glaze in his eyes, and I'm sure I don't want to know him anymore. He is lost behind a glass wall, seemingly here, but not. What else looks like that? Sometimes drunkenness or sorrow. I become discouraged then. I know there is nothing here for me, too many needles welded to too many hearts.

"Fuck you," I say to whoever might be listening. But no one is paying attention, just like no one has looked outside and noticed the dead cat. How could they miss it?

I ditch the party, give up on finding something in this place. I don't say "thank you" or "goodbye" to anyone as I make my way across the room, which smells of spilled beer. I glide through the crowd as if I'm not even here, past the whirr of the blender and people laughing. I walk down the dusty warehouse steps, several stories to the street. Then I pause outside the door to catch my breath.

For a moment, I consider going down to the falls to fish the cat out of the water. I could put his fat body in a box, take him back upstairs to the party and call it art. Found object. I'd title it "No Swimming on a Full Stomach," and laugh at my own joke. I could glue a side-view mirror to the outside of the box and paint in small letters, "Objects in mirror are closer to death than they appear." People might look at themselves in the mirror and fix their hair. Maybe they'd get high and think it was profound. It would make a statement. I can picture all of this as clearly as if I were there.

Traffic passes behind me, and I turn in time to see an old white bomb of a Buick round the corner and disappear. Another night I might've thought it was Oliver's car, but tonight I am tired of believing things that aren't true. One day I'd like to believe in possibility again, nurse it back to health, have something like faith. But for now I'm worn out.

After the funeral, some people said if Oliver hadn't been a junkie he would've been a barfly. But I knew he'd gotten sober once for a period of time. He was full of life and learned to ice skate that winter. He said, "Jane, don't give up before the miracles happen." He said, "There's more than one." It wasn't original—he was quoting someone—but it made him happy for a while to think that change required no effort, that it was simply a miracle, and for that reason, things would stay fixed. I remember he was skating very slowly when he said it, one skate in front of the other, trying to draw a figure eight.

"You need to make the circle connect," I said, pointing to the top of the eight.

"I'm *trying*," he answered, a bit annoyed with me, as if I'd missed the point. I cross the bridge leading away from the warehouse party. The bridge is covered in graffiti and weeds. I stand at the railing for a long time and look down into the river. The water is laden with so much debris it looks like solid ground. Then I spot the cat, its balloon of a body floating in the river, almost buried by the garbage. He's puffed up, except for his tail; his ears are pointed down into the water like he's listening to faint voices, to the call of something deep below. How could this have happened? But I already know.

I watch the shit roll through, slow and steady. The river is an arm of the reservoir, a vein running through the city. I wonder if it's possible to track a single drop of water as it travels through the jumble. I wonder how long it takes to emerge on the other side.

Lawrence Loves Somebody on Pratt Street

When I come to the door, Aunt Gloria's got her rosary in one hand, thumbing through it like she's shelling beans. She says she saw it on the TV about Lawrence's unit. "They been hit over there in that big sand pit," she says. She wipes at her eyes with a tissue. Then she rocks forward in her chair for momentum and leans all her weight on her cane to lift herself up. She hobbles over to the TV.

"Aunt Gloria, don't you get up. Make JJ switch the channel for you. He's sitting right there."

Aunt Gloria don't say nothing. She changes the channel and waits for the next news to say something different. She wants the first news to be a mistake. I stand there in the doorway and watch the news with her. We don't speculate much out loud but inside I know we're both wondering about Lawrence and if he's still alive. But we're quiet with JJ in the room. JJ sits in the corner on the floor looking at his car magazines and telling stories to hisself. He can't read except a few words and his mind's not right on account of huffing shoe polish when he was little. Now he's thirty-six but that don't mean nothing.

"Maybe Lawrence is OK," I say to Aunt Gloria. "We don't know. Maybe he'll call."

"Maybe he will," she says. "God help us if there's two soldiers come knock on our door. That's when we know there's bad news for certain. In the meantime we pray."

Then she starts to hum her favorite hymn under her breath, "A Mighty Fortress Is Our God," and gently rocks herself in her chair even though it don't move. It's like that song is her oxygen.

"That's right," I say and reach out to hold her hand with the bent fingers that're curled up like a bird's claw.

When my two kids come running inside from playing on the porch, Aunt Gloria don't say nothing more about Lawrence. She tells me, "Wanda, go down to Ditto's Lounge and get us a pizza for dinner. We need something." She reaches for her pocketbook, which she keeps on the floor right next to her chair. She gets out her change purse and hands me a couple of dollars. "And, a course," she whispers, "get us a order of onion rings," and she nods her head toward you know who.

JJ looks up. "Rings!" he says. "I want rings!" He suddenly stirs away from his car magazine.

"Onion rings!" my two boys join in. They're young, four and five, and they jump on JJ and try to tickle him. "Onion rings!" they laugh.

But JJ don't like when they bother his things. He says, "Stop!" and gets a look because they wrinkled his magazine. "Stop!" he says again. My kids get in fights with JJ all the time. They play with the same toys, the robots and the plastic soldiers because they're mentally about the same age, except JJ could throw them against the wall if he wanted to.

"Mind your uncle," I say. "Stop jumping," and then I leave out the front door and go down to Ditto's to get us a pizza. I don't even order myself a drink in the bar, but instead I wait outside against the brick wall. I watch the cars pass on Lombard Street and beyond that, I see these boys who are older than mine, roaming the streets in a pack, a couple of them on bicycles that they got from somewheres. They're going to be bad news when they get older, I can tell. I say a little good luck prayer for them and cross my fingers that somehow they get straightened up. Or get out some other way.

We was just kids when Aunt Gloria gathered all us up. First me, Lawrence, and Kinny, then later our cousin, JJ. Aunt Gloria come to our old house with her shopping cart and a handful of plastic bags for our clothes and toys. She made us wear our winter coats and told us to follow her out. Our parents were gone anyway, so we went to her house where she had real curtains in the front window, not just a sheet, and some flowers in a jar on the table and she had a tiny fenced-in backyard for us to play in.

She got JJ because his daddy roamed the streets and got hisself arrested a few times. JJ's daddy would lock JJ in the closet to keep him safe. Except there was tins of shoe polish in a box, and you can guess what happened with it. JJ was just nearly a baby when he did that. He didn't know no better. But a course, it affected his head and he's been slow ever since.

JJ's daddy—Aunt Gloria's brother, Al—he ended up homeless, and ever once in a while we see him. The last time we seen Al, about five or six years ago, he was out on the street asking cars for money. He might be dead now, we don't know. Our parents were practically the same. But then Daddy died first and Mama run off to Chicago, and a few years later we got notice that she was found dead too. At least we know.

It must of been a heartbreak for Aunt Gloria to see all these little kids, her nieces and nephews, without nothing. She raised us and combed our hair and made us go to school. We listened to Aunt Gloria, and both me and Lawrence graduated from high school (except, me in the same year as Lawrence because I flunked twice).

She had a harder time with Kinny. But Kinny is getting his GED now and working as a mechanic's apprentice. When he was a boy, he was real friendly. He'd talk to just about anyone. He'd follow people around and not even know them, or else he'd roam on his own and get lost. You'd turn for one second and Kinny'd be gone.

One day me and Lawrence and Aunt Gloria went looking for him, knocking on doors and asking neighbors to send Kinny home. Me and Lawrence, we was about eight and ten and Aunt Gloria held both us tight by the hand even though we was too old for hand-holding. But she wouldn't let us go and I could tell it wasn't a good idea to fight against her. She walked us down the streets where we was not allowed to be by ourselves. We passed this boarded house that got spray painted in big letters. *RIP Hanky.* On the sidewalk there was balloons and a stuffed bear and candy boxes and lighters and empty cartons of cigarettes and dried-up candles. By then me and Lawrence knew what RIP meant. We seen it in other places, makeshift altars on crumbling walls. But I still stopped to look.

I bent down and reached toward the stuffed bear. Aunt Gloria yanked my hand. "Wanda, that ain't yours. That belongs to some dumbass that got themselves shot." She sounded angry when she said it. "They gone and joined the Stupid Club," she spit. I was quiet for a few steps. Then Aunt Gloria stopped in the middle of the sidewalk and turned to face us. She was fuming, like we was in trouble just for wanting a bear, and she said, "Lawrence, Wanda, I never want to see neither one of you get yourself in with a gang. I ain't never going to a funeral for drugs." Lawrence and me just looked at each other, but Aunt Gloria didn't wait for us to say nothing. She charged up the hill pulling us by the hand, looking and hollering for Kinny.

Now I realize that's the one time I got a glimpse of what Aunt Gloria must of felt about her brother Al and our parents. She told us they loved us when they was alive. But she's got this secret other side that's angry.

Kinny's got this secret side, too. Something happened a year ago and he got real serious. Now he's trying to stay out of trouble. That means he comes inside at night, away from the streets, to hang with the family, which is me and JJ and Aunt Gloria and my two boys. And Lawrence before Lawrence joined the Army. Kinny don't say much and is strict with my boys, sometimes for no reason. He's got something inside him that don't know how to get out, and he's got a hole in his side where he been shot once. Now the hole is all growed over, a bump on his skin that's raised like he's got a grape underneath, or an eyeball. He seen everything in a whole new way. He's lucky Aunt Gloria let him back in the house. She don't put up with foolishness.

When the onion rings and pizza are ready, I take the steaming box home to Aunt Gloria and JJ and my boys. Then Kinny comes in from his job, all greasy in his mechanic jumpsuit, and we eat slices of peperoni pizza on paper plates and drink red punch. Aunt Gloria and me, we don't say nothing out of the ordinary. We act like it is just another day. Later, we tell Kinny what we heard on the TV and he just nods slowly and don't say nothing.

After dinner, the boys wrestle in the living room and we watch TV just like any other night. But everything in the house is got an air of waiting, like it's holding its breath.

Pretty soon, Kinny goes upstairs and takes a shower and turns in early.

Then I put my boys to bed and Aunt Gloria hobbles into her room and she shuts the door. But I seen the light underneath and I know she's reading the Bible. After a while, JJ goes down into the basement to his cot and then it's just me.

I dust Lawrence's picture we got hanging on the wall. And the other one propped up on top of the radiator, the one where he's all handsome in his dress uniform. I think how proud we all was. We thrown a party for him before he got shipped out, but it wasn't that many people come except us. Lawrence always keeps to hisself. He reads a lot and wants to go to school when he gets out the Army. That's what keeps him going. He don't have a girlfriend.

Except this one time when we was teenagers. He had a crush on this girl named Skinny Lisa for a long time. One day, Aunt Gloria come home from work in a huff. She sank down in the green chair and propped her feet up on the hassock and said, "Lawrence, who do you know on Pratt Street?"

Lawrence shrugged his shoulders. "I don't know."

"That's not what I hear," Aunt Gloria said.

Kinny and I sneaked a peek at Lawrence. We knew all about Skinny Lisa. But we didn't know what Lawrence might of done with her to get Aunt Gloria mad.

Aunt Gloria said, "I seen it scrawled in marker on a garage door in the alley: *Lawrence loves somebody on Pratt Street.*"

"I didn't write that," Lawrence mumbled and looked down at his hands. "That was somebody else."

"Is it true?" Aunt Gloria leaned forward to grab him by the pant leg in case he tried to squirm away.

"I didn't write it," Lawrence said again.

Kinny coughed. I knew who did it, but I didn't say nothing and neither did Lawrence. We figured Aunt Gloria would explode through the roof if she found out one of us was writing graffiti.

"Is it true you love somebody on Pratt Street?" Then she laughed and laughed. "There's nothing wrong with more love in this world," she said. "You give Lisa my regards."

Kinny and I looked up, surprised. We didn't know whether to laugh or bust on Lawrence. But Lawrence was even more surprised and mostly embarrassed.

"There are worse things that could be writ on walls about you," Aunt Gloria said. "But I'm guessing somebody you know wrote it, so you might as well clean it up," she said. "And take Kinny with you." Then she let go of Lawrence's leg and slapped Kinny on the back of his head, not hard, but hard enough to let him know he should of knowed better.

That's what I think about now, while I wonder if Lawrence is been hit by a bullet or a bomb. He's so far away now, it don't seem real. I know it's painted over but I want to get out of here, see if his name is still on that garage door. See for sure that my brother lived here in this neighborhood with us, and that he loved some girl enough for all of us to know it.

I wander around the house and pick things off the floor. First my boys' clothes and toys, and then I reach down and pick up these little pieces of lint and carpet, like I never seen them before. And while I'm down there, I see little specs of sand that my boys must of brought in from the playground and I start on my hands and knees, like they're the most important things in the world for me to pick up, these little grains. I gather them in my palm like I'm supposed to put them back in the playground to keep the sand pile from disappearing. So I pick them up, one little grain at a time, and maybe it hardly makes a difference to the world if they're missing, but on the other hand, I say to myself, if all these little grains got carried off one by one, they wouldn't be nothing left.

Stray

Rayburn kisses me hello in the parking lot. He says, "How's my stray from Ellijay?" then sticks his tongue in my mouth.

"I'm dying in the heat," I tell him.

We're somewhere outside of Nashville, off the interstate next to a Waffle House; there's a Texaco across the street. We could be anywhere, lost in a maze of parking lots that don't connect, too many curbs in the way. Except here there are ugly yellow lights flashing in the middle of the afternoon, pointing the way to the Music City Inn.

I'm steamed because Rayburn was late and I don't have air conditioning in my car, just vinyl seats that stick to my thighs. While I was waiting for him to show, I dumped my purse trying to find the right lipstick. I decided orange for Rayburn. But the color I wanted had softened in all the heat, like a melted chocolate bar. When I tried to touch up my lips, the little wand broke off and smudged my teeth. I blotted my lips on the tiny map to this exit that Rayburn had scribbled for me.

Rayburn is easy about getting us a room and he pays for it, no question. He winks at me from across the parking lot as he opens the office door, like he knows how to keep a secret. I stand outside by my beat-up tan Escort and pull my bags out of the trunk. I watch the tractor-trailers across the road at the gas station as they strain to move forward, like fat-bellied beasts, trotting and snorting toward the highway.

Rayburn unlocks a room around back, indistinguishable from the room next to it, from any other motel: four cups wrapped in plastic, short white towels hung in the bathroom, flower pictures above the beds. The first thing I do is turn on the cold air because it's still hot as hell outside even though the sun has clouded over. I'm determined to cool off, and I have my eye on the blue pool glowing in the middle of the parking lot I spotted while I was waiting for Rayburn. There's no stopping me, and I guess Rayburn realizes it. I change into a black netted one-piece, a stylish thing, revealing and classic, which I look great in. I know this.

I parade across the black pavement in my suit and black leather sandals, a purple fringed scarf tied around my waist. Rayburn follows and sits patiently while I fawn over myself, adjust my sunglasses, move the chaise longue. It is a show. I'm pretending to be the lover of his dreams. Rayburn is just happy he's talked a woman nearly twenty-five years younger into meeting him. He'll listen to me say anything.

"It's a shame it's cloudy; I wish the sun was out," I say, as if he could change that for me. Somehow it's befitting. I wanted this to be a vacation day, but it's not exactly right. I'm swimming in some dinky motel pool after driving three hours to this exit (not even in Nashville) to meet a man I've been flirting with for a few weeks. Rayburn doesn't get it: the sad state of our lives, the hilarity of him sitting in the clouds for me.

He isn't bad for fifty-six, I think, though his breath is slightly sour when I kiss him. It's those cigars he says he doesn't smoke often. I wonder if he can taste the cigarettes I tell him I don't smoke. It's one of many secrets I keep from him, just like the wife he doesn't mention to me. We flirt like this with each other but I don't consider it lying unless I get caught and can't talk my way out of it. My husband is back in Ellijay and it seems unlikely this will catch up with me.

I watch Rayburn in his chair pretending to read his Civil War book, the Battle of something. He's got green eyes with crow's feet, eyes that hide things. He's tan and bowlegged, but it's his toenails that are old. I try not to think about them, but they're brown and gnarled like burned-out tree stumps.

Of course, Rayburn is no slouch. He's charmed me here in his own way. This doctor from Kentucky with his slick Lincoln parked in front of our turquoise motel door. He knew which exit to tell me to get off, which parking lot to wait in. Turn right at the flashing trailer sign. He's done this before.

I tell Rayburn how I'd swim all day, every day if I had a pool in my backyard. The water still holds me like it did when I was young, when my brother and I swam regularly at the community pool. For as tan as he is, Rayburn doesn't like to swim, but I dive to the bottom of the pool and hold my breath as long as I can. Rayburn is trying to tell me something and I don't want to hear it.

I come up for a quick breath and dive back under because he's starting to say the thing again. I love the thick silence water makes so sounds can't touch me. It's an escape I learned as a child. When my mother called for us, my brother Lenny and I would swim to the bottom pretending not to hear. We were all muscle then and we could sink.

But I can't hold air for long, so when I surface, Rayburn points to a sign and says, "Swim at your own risk, sweet girl. No lifeguards on duty!" He is trying to be cute when there is nothing to talk about. *What's your name? Choo-choo train*, my father used to say in a low voice on the phone to his secret lover. Fluff between the sex. Rayburn chuckles, "Don't worry, I'll save you if you go under." He can't swim a stroke, can't even tread water. I float on my back and look up at the clouds. My ears are underwater and I pretend I don't see him. I know he won't save me from anything. That's not why I'm here.

When I finally get out of the pool, I tell Rayburn he's lucky I haven't pushed him in the deep end. "We even made our pets swim when we were growing up," I say. I'm dripping on everything, on Rayburn and his book. He's got this mole on his cheek and I look at it when I talk to him. "We had some guinea pigs that died of pneumonia because Lenny and I tried to teach them to swim," I say. Rayburn snorts. He thinks I'm being cute.

My brother and I just wanted to see what would happen. We filled a bucket with water to clean their aquarium, and I guess I was feeling mean, so I dropped them in the water. They sank straight to the bottom. Tiny bubbles rose up from their noses.

"Like you would do, Rayburn," I tease him.

The guinea pigs didn't float like we thought they would. They didn't rise to the surface, so Lenny scooped them out and saved them from drowning. We held them in our t-shirts and put them on the picnic table to dry in the sun. The guinea pigs didn't move for a long time. They were stunned and barely breathing, shaken from the glass walls of their miniature world. I felt ashamed. Life cannot be the same after something like that. I understood that the day I found a love note in my mother's slip drawer. I carried it around for a while: the weight of someone else's secret.

I didn't want to look at Lenny, so I said it quietly, afraid of what might come next. "You know Mom is having an affair," I said.

"Yeah," he answered. He petted one of the guinea pigs with a dry spot on his shirt. "With Harry Vernon."

"That dumbass," I said, relieved. I didn't have to hate him by myself anymore.

I don't tell Rayburn any of this. I don't tell him about the silk underclothes my mother kept folded over a copy of *The Joy of Sex*, nor about the note that said, "I love you because you always know when to stop and never do," scrawled in Harry Vernon's stupid handwriting. Rayburn doesn't want to know where I've been. We do not want to see each other's insides. He just likes the results that got me to this motel, straddling his body with my legs. He's sweet and limp and I masturbate while he takes a shower.

Since his wife kicked him out, Lenny sleeps in the cab of his tractor-trailer. It's like a tiny apartment in there, with his mattress and sleeping bag. He tells me how he unhooks the trailer and drives the cab to the Laundromat and takes up too many spaces in the parking lot while he washes his jeans and towels. He grins at the tired woman who runs the coin-op laundry and gets away with it. Lenny can smile and wink and make women feel flattered. I envy him, that he can travel and leave, change his place for a while.

My husband hasn't thrown me out yet. It will be for good when it comes. There has been the coldest silence growing in him like a tumor. The two of us are waiting for I don't know what—a snap, maybe, to pull us out of this trance. But as cold as I am to him sometimes, I'm not strong enough to let go. So I've learned to talk my way out of everything, which is its own trap. If I grovel enough, I can ease my way back into the lull that makes me want to leave.

For a while I hung with a young guy who did karate or one of those and would tell me about breaking boards. He said the way to do it is to visualize what is beyond the board, look through the board and it will break. What I understood was that if someone looked hard enough at me, I would become invisible and my lies would split apart.

If my husband knows things, he doesn't say. He eats his fish sticks with quiet manners and leaves his dinner plate on the coffee table while the catsup gets hard. At night, he sits with the television on and flips through his music book, playing pieces of songs on his saxophone until he hits a wrong note and starts over.

Rayburn's got a Lincoln with comfortable cloth seats. He drives us all over Nashville. I glance over at him and there are filaments of hair growing from the sides of his ears. Sweet little wisps. It doesn't bother me. He drives me by Vanderbilt, where he went to medical school. I can see him remembering things. He says he was not second in his class, he was somewhere near the bottom. "It was a struggle," he says. He tells me about being a doctor in Vietnam, about being at such and such a lateral, then being moved, north or south, I don't know.

He's traveled all over: to Thailand twice and Wyoming. You can see what the appeal is for me. If my husband throws me out, maybe I'll go to one of these places. Rayburn keeps talking but I look over at myself in the side-view mirror. I've got my sunglasses on and I've pinned my hair up in a roll, streaks of my dark roots mixed with the red. I'm wearing an orange cotton dress, fitting and long (no underwear, of course), and I've chosen a deep maroon-colored lipstick. I'm slinky and charming.

He drives me around the city and I cross my legs to reveal my tanned calf muscles. He pats my knee occasionally like he can't believe his luck.

In the motel room, we lean on some pillows and drink Clos du Bois out of motel cups. I picked this wine at the liquor store because I liked the label, which promised to be better but it leaves a lousy taste. Rayburn is drunk and amorous and leans over to say sloppy words in my year. He's struggling to keep my attention, but I've turned on the television, the eleven o'clock news to keep the mood stale. There's a commercial for used cars, then another for puppy chow; dogs and puppies bounce across the screen.

Rayburn says, "That reminds me of your guinea pigs, the one's you killed, you mean girl!"

"We didn't kill them," I say, and punch Rayburn in the arm for bringing it up. But I wonder. They were pets that Harry Vernon had given us. Harry Vernon kept animals in his basement and let Lenny play with them while Mom sat upstairs listening to jazz and drinking wine. Harry Vernon bottled wine from the grapes he pressed, and when his guinea pigs had babies, he let Lenny pick out two. "We didn't kill them! We saved them from drowning!" I say.

"You can save my life anytime you want, sweet stray girl," Rayburn says. Then, "Save me! Save me!" and he grabs my body and pulls me closer.

"Save your own sorry ass."

I'm tired; this isn't fun for me anymore.

The man on the news is talking about a carjacking, about a woman being shot in the head in a parking lot. "It's tragic," says the anchorman, and he bows his head slightly with an expression of concern. Then he starts in on the five-day weather forecast.

"It's tragic," says Rayburn, and he sticks his tongue in my ear.

"God, Rayburn!" I yell. Then, sweetly, "Roll over, close your eyes."

I reach down and grab my purse from the side of the bed and dump it out on the mattress.

"Can I open my eyes yet?"

"Not yet," I say. He thinks I'm flirting. I find the lipstick I want, a nice purple blue, and I lean over him with my hair brushing his face as if this is all part of the seduction.

"How about now?" he asks hopefully.

"Just wait." I unroll my lipstick and smear it on his lips, past his lips and around the sides. I dot the mole on his cheek. "There. You're done."

He looks ridiculous. His lips are purple blue, as if he's been shivering in the water too long. His face is pruned with wrinkles. He could be a corpse.

"How do I look?" he asks, and smacks his lips together. He doesn't get it, how pathetic he is.

"You don't want to know."

"Oh, look!" he says, sitting up to look in the mirror across from the bed. "I'm a clown!"

Rayburn is asleep and I get up early to swim. It's eight a.m., but there is already someone else out by the pool, a skinny little boy with purple popsicle stains around his mouth and down his belly. His mother and her lover are off under one of the umbrella tables. I can tell it's her lover by the way they don't mind the child, by the way she leans in as she talks. They aren't listening to each other, but they are soft about pretending it and behind their eyes they're alive and wired, breathing heavy with every feel. I know these things.

I dive in the pool and open my eyes. Being underwater, inside it, is smooth and cold. There are no edges to what I see. I somersault and blow bubbles from my nose before I swim to the side and pull myself out. Then I pat myself dry with a small, white motel towel and stretch out in a chaise longue waiting for the sun to burn off the morning. The other woman is laughing with her lover. Her voice is low and smokey. The little boy hums like an engine for his toy boat.

I nap lightly until I feel a splash on my legs from someone jumping in. I open my eyes thinking it's Rayburn trying to impress me, but it's the boy, no more than four, in the deep end, going under. He's got his boat in his hands and is calm in the water as he sinks, but of course I jump from my chair. I know full well he can't swim. I kneel on the side of the pool and plunge my arm into the water up to my shoulder, trying to grab him. I reach farther so my face is underwater, my eyes are open, and I can see to pull him up by his armpit. The cement tears the skin on my knees, but I've got him. I hold him out of the water and hug him. His mother has just realized something has happened and she comes running toward us and startles the boy so he starts screaming. He's yelping and coughing as she takes him from my arms. She's got black circles around her eyes from heavy mascara left on all night. I think, *now the kid will never learn to swim, he's so scared.*

She says thank you, then turns quickly and walks back to the umbrella table while her son screams. She doesn't look at my face. On another day we might've nodded to each other in passing, maybe smiled at something in absolute understanding. She doesn't realize we're the same, and maybe we're not. As it is, I found her out when she didn't want to get caught. She rocks her son in her lap and kisses his head. Her lover has put on his flip-flops and is walking across the parking lot back toward their turquoise door.

I want to say my own life has not been without shame. But there is no one for me to explain this to.

Small Deaths

It's silent where I stand, the silence of winter. I've hiked far into the woods, up to my calves in deep snow, while everything is white and black, dark and wet, the trees half exposed, half buried. The only thing I hear is the sound of my own breath and the crunching of the snow under my boots; ahead of me a crow is cawing. I follow it, let it lead me. I watch for the bird overhead, and by the time I lose sight of the crow, I'm close to a stream. Pillows of snow swell next to the water, sculpted to the bank as if to cushion the flow. The stream is more hushed than usual, but I listen closely as the water trickles over rocks. There is chatter, quiet conversation underneath, voices and whispers at a distance like the sound of a funeral, people speaking with concern.

I look across the stream where a spot of light catches my eye. I can't see clearly, but I think there's a drop of water—snow melting from the branch of a bush—that shimmers in the sun and wind. This droplet blinks at me from across the stream and changes colors, a small sequin sparkling as if to tell me something, to speak in code. It reminds me of the crystal necklace you wore, the one I wrapped around your neck after you died. I stand by the stream for a long time and concentrate on the bead of light, sure no one else has seen it or will, its presence dependent on luck and the right time of day, the angle of the sun, a person in a path to witness it. This drop is a moment, and I watch it as long as it exists. I listen with the invisible part of myself that understands these things. I say "Hello" to you out loud.

We'd been watching television. It was a game show, because I remember questions about Russia, and I was thinking of Siberia and snow, but I was too tired to play the game out loud. We'd been camped together for weeks, lying in bed, holding hands. I thought, *if I close my eyes for just a minute I won't miss much.* I might've already started dreaming.

That's when you tapped me on the shoulder. "Honey, please help me to the bathroom," you said. Or maybe you just said, "Honey," and I already knew what you meant because we'd been through the routine so many times. I came around to your side of the bed and eased you out, your legs as unsteady as a colt first trying to stand. You were wearing the silk pajamas I bought you when you first got sick. I thought they would give grace to your dying, make you feel beautiful or dignified. I hadn't considered that soon there'd be stains on the silk, brown spots of dried blood that would leak out of your mouth when you coughed or vomited. I hadn't counted on that; nor did I know that stains on silk would make your illness even more affronting. There was so much I learned the wrong way.

When you died, for instance. I didn't notice at first because I was wiping your mouth, the long strings of spit that reached down to the toilet, like spider webs so thin and hard to break. I was cleaning your chin with toilet paper and telling you to spit. It was the last thing I said, "Spit!" And then I realized I didn't hear your breath, the puddle sound of phlegm and fluid in your lungs. I looked at your face to find out what had happened, because there had been no sigh or suddenness.

I was holding up all your weight. I had my arm tight around your shoulders because you'd been too weak to spit or stand. Sometimes you were so frail I had to put my finger in your mouth to clear out all the extra pieces of vomit, like soft mud. It was disgusting, but I did it, and I would've done it again.

But you were not there. You had gone. For a moment I wondered if I still needed to put my finger in your mouth, or hand you a glass of water and say, "Here, Mom. Rinse." That was part of our routine, too. Then it occurred to me while I was holding you that something in the distance had finally become real. Death was no longer somewhere else, another week, a few days away.

You became much heavier in my arms when I realized it, and yet I couldn't let go. I wanted to put you back in bed, drag you into the next room where you could rest, but your body wouldn't cooperate, slumping as though you were drugged, had fallen fast asleep. I had no choice; I had to lower you onto the bathroom floor. I didn't want to leave you there. I wanted to clean you up, comb your hair, make you look nice. For what? For when I made phone calls and let everyone know?

I looked in the mirror and straightened my own hair then. I was preparing both of us, I guess, for what would come next. I saw myself and started crying very quietly, just for a moment. When I tried to pick you up again, you'd become much heavier. I felt like I was dragging a drunk, misshapen and inelegant. Your feet slid sideways, gathering the bathroom rug. "This isn't funny, Mother," I said.

It was and it wasn't. We had howled at the clumsiness of death for the last several weeks. Once, we couldn't stop laughing when I wiped vomit from your chin and pieces of toilet paper stuck to your face like a beard. It was absurd, and we couldn't breathe even when you said your stomach hurt and you started crying. We laughed at this dying and let it be an awkward forgiveness between us.

But that evening I was alone with the humor and tragedy, and I hadn't been able to pull you very far in the bathroom, perhaps two feet. I wished you'd been there to see it with me. "Such a nice-sized bathroom," we often said, yet when I tried to carry you from it, it seemed the door was unreachable, the bedroom miles away. I held you by the armpits; you'd lost a lot of weight, and I could feel how thin your bones were, as though your skeleton was waiting to come out. I dragged you with your bottom sinking toward the floor, your foot and the rug getting caught on the hamper, and I apologized, afraid I was hurting you, as if you'd turn purple and bruise. Your head rolled to the side, and when I looked in the mirror I saw both of us: a portrait of Mother and Daughter. And Death. It stopped me, and I had to rest you on the floor again.

I sat on the floor next to you, less eager to tuck you back in bed and begin the next round of events. I remember I looked around me then: there were things in the bathroom—tiny specks of mold dotting the faucet like freckles, and the towel rack coming loose from the wall—things that came alive for me, grew into existence suddenly. I looked at you, and I guess I hadn't noticed the moles on your neck or how thin your hair had gotten around your ears. I hadn't seen you wear earrings in so long. We had talked about that: which earrings you wanted to wear for the funeral, and I couldn't remember if you'd said gold or mother of pearl. I hadn't been paying enough attention. The routine of your sickness had become ordinary to me, and most likely I'd been thinking of something else, of feeding the cats or getting home to my own house for a rest and a shower. In the end, I decided on your favorite gold hoops for the undertaker. I kept the mother-of-pearl teardrops for myself.

And the shoes? I always loved the shoes in your closet, standing in rows, as though invisible women were waiting to dance. And so many pretty clothes. But I knew you weren't going to look like yourself in the coffin no matter what you were wearing. The embalmers would make you into an imitation of yourself, with too much rouge and eye shadow: Death gussied up as Life, dozing in a coffin.

While you rested on the bathroom floor, the house seemed shockingly still. Even the television in the other room was far off, keeping track of the time with commercials. You'd died, but things had continued without pause. The sink in front of me was beating out its own time, dripping like it had for years, marking the passage with a rust stain on the porcelain. I found large balls of dust and hair caught in the corners of the bathroom that had been growing with your illness. I should've cleaned them for you; I meant to.

But what I did next: I straightened the rug and pushed the hamper to the side and made more room on the floor so I could lie next to you on the cool tile. Then I placed my head on your stomach like I did when I was your baby. The thump of your heart was missing, that was all.

Life for both of us had evaporated, had been disappearing gradually for months. Those microscopic moments, one dying into the next, all of them led to this spot where I stand in the snow, listening to the trickle of water, to the spirits chattering with each other while the chill of the wind reaches my bones.

I don't know what made me lie down with you—perhaps one last chance to pay attention—but it was gone as soon as I dragged you from the bathroom, propped you in bed and picked up the phone. It went on from there. That time on the bathroom floor was the part I hadn't been able to explain when they asked me. I told them how we held hands and watched TV, all the years resting between us. I told them that. But the rest was mine: the cold tile giving me chills, my backbone pressed against the floor. It was remarkable, the view from there, the underside of things. I knew I would never see from that same place again. Above us the brown water stain on the ceiling almost looked like billowing clouds.

Camera Obscura: Light Seeps In

Take a picture of this: a woman in her backyard holding an old tin cracker box, aiming it, you might say, at another woman, who stands beyond the fence with her face peeping through the slats. They don't talk, but they stay very still for maybe twenty minutes, a half hour.

The woman who's holding the box is tall and somewhat stylish and would be more attractive if she were friendly. She is someone who, when her neighbors wave hello, looks to the ground to avoid talking. If she does talk, she's shy and brief with her words, as if she's in a hurry and doesn't know what to say. Once in a while you get a sense there is something greater on her mind, something she would almost say, but doesn't. She darts inside her house and closes the door and her neighbors take it to mean she's aloof. For a while, there was a man who came to her house, a boyfriend she dated for a time; the neighbors speculated, but no one knew for sure.

The other woman, the one behind the fence, is an old prostitute who's seen better days. Her hair is oily and dyed black; her pantyhose have long runs and are baggy around the ankles; the heels of her shoes are scuffed nubs. She's often seen walking around the block, looking for company. A woman who has no one to talk to, so she talks to everyone.

How is it these two women are out here facing each other, like opposite sides of the same coin? Something occurs to the prostitute and she starts talking, but the bony one looks alarmed, like the exposure is too much for her and she must go inside, back to whatever life it is she has there. *Hold that thought; I'll be right back*, she wants to say.

Here's another snapshot—we'll call it "Pining after Him." On a different day, the same skinny woman (Roberta) is sitting on her bedroom floor eating ice cream directly from the container and wearing nothing but a ratty t-shirt and some underwear. The room is dark. Wadded tissues litter her floor like paper flowers. She plays a song on her cassette recorder—the same song a million times a day—and sways back and forth with the music. She scoops more ice cream and shivers.

"All kinds of trouble but there's only one lonely," she sings with her mouth full. She tries to imitate the sorrowful lilt of the singer's voice. Her neighbors have heard her through the walls. "But there's only one lonely," she sings. Roberta loves the refrain. If she were a lounge singer, she'd belt it out every night, and the audience would marvel; they would cry, too. But what does it mean—only one lonely? Is she singing as if she's the only one who's alone? Or as though there's just one kind of loneliness? No matter: she's singing the wrong words. Roberta rewinds the cassette and plays the song again. She sings soulfully into her ice cream. The real words: "You're my only one and only," the title of the song, but that's not what Roberta hears.

Outside her window, someone else is bellowing: the man next door who sits in his car and listens to the radio. He annoys Roberta until she finally closes her window and turns on a fan to block the noise. Sometimes she'd like to pound her fist through the wall and strangle the people on the other side, tell them to shut up with all their thumping and bumping. She's not fond of her neighbors and would like to blame them for a lot of things, even the end of her last relationship, though they had nothing to do with it.

That's Roberta's story: the way she misinterprets love. She misconstrues men's words, mistrusts, mistakes, misunderstands. Her love life is sparse and introverted. It's not often she meets men who are attracted to shy, silent, willowy types, which is how she sees herself. When she does date, she has tragic taste, and usually finds a man who is content with the idea of a woman. Not exactly fertile ground for love, but Roberta keeps hoping for something beyond average. Nothing happens to her worse than anyone else, but she is easily devastated.

For instance, the last man who broke up with her: he's gathering his shirts from Roberta's closet, his socks on the floor, his dirty boxers that mix in the basket with hers (their underwear is closer than they are). Then he pulls open the drawer of the nightstand and removes the box of condoms. "You won't be needing these, Charlotte," he says.

Roberta is stunned. He's called her by his ex-wife's name *and* he's taking the condoms. She doesn't know what to say. It's clear he's on his way to his next girlfriend. Roberta looks away, then bends down to pluck a piece of lint. She pets the cat that sleeps on the floor. She picks it up and carries it around, desperately holding on as the cat squirms and claws to get away.

"One can always use condoms," he says while he stuffs the square plastic wrappers into his pocket like penny candies. "They make good water balloons," he laughs. What an imbecile. But Roberta supposes this is his attempt to explain himself and divert her from the evidence of his leaving. She bites her thumbnail instead of calling him an asshole. She watches him grab a bunch of over-ripe bananas off the kitchen counter before he opens the door.

Roberta is swirling in a tunnel and can't see his face when he turns to say goodbye and something else. She's frozen, and all she can see is his back and the bulge in his pocket as he walks down the front steps, a pocket full of condoms. She watches as he stops and talks to one of her neighbors, the man in the car; he hands him a banana before getting in his own car and pulling away. Her neighbor waves to her, unaware of what has just occurred; he waves to her and jams the banana in his mouth with his other hand. Roberta slams the door.

She knows she should tear her ex-lover's name out of her phone book, but instead she dreams up excuses to call a few days later. She dials him, then holds her breath while the phone rings, almost hoping he doesn't answer. Don't do it, she tells herself. There's still a chance she could hang up, and she debates this while the phone rings again. She waits. It rings. And then he answers.

"Hey," she says, and is silent for a few moments. The phone is hot against her ear. "Listen…" She wants to sound nonchalant instead of heartsick. "I called last night but didn't get an answer. I thought maybe something happened," she says. "I thought maybe something happened to you." She doesn't really want to hear him speak, but until he does, she stays on the line.

"I was out," he tells her. This response opens a whole well of questions Roberta could ask.

"Oh," she says.

"We'll go to the movies one night," he assures her.

For a long time, she believes him. She has hope based on her view of things, which is inverted from fact. This breakup heckles her for longer than necessary, diminishing her confidence. It might make more sense if this great melancholy happened when Roberta was, say, seventeen. But she's forty-three when she collapses on her bedroom floor and sings the wrong words into her spoon.

"It's no problem," she says to the mirror. She winks at herself as if she's strong. At night, between the hours when she paces her apartment and is tempted to call him, she watches her neighbors across the alley, their marriage as it happens under the kitchen lights. She strains to hear them speak.

Sometimes she tries on all the clothes in her closet. She rummages through past boyfriends in this manner, as outfits she's forgotten or outgrown. She models for the mirror. This is who she used to be, muted orange coat with pearl buttons. Pink angora sweater. Green dress with rhinestones that she bought at a thrift store, a dress that never fit well, acquired during Boyfriend K years when everything was the wrong size.

The clothes pile up on her bed, shadows of herself. She doesn't throw anything away, just folds them neatly and tucks them back into the nest of her closet as if she's a momma bird keeping her eggs safe, waiting for something to hatch. Meanwhile, she sits alone, warming each fragile infatuation with diligence.

Outside Roberta's apartment, the old prostitute sits on a stoop across the street. She polishes her shoes with spit. She licks her fingers, then shines the scuffs as if they'll disappear. Neighbors call her Betty, as in Betty Boop, a joke born from her black bob. No one knows her real name. Often she sits across the street from Frank, the guy who sings in his car. She ogles him with her mournful eyes, spends hours gazing in his direction. He can't stand it.

Roberta finds Frank just as bothersome when he sings love songs to himself and to the women on the street. Roberta can rarely leave her house without a show. When Frank's not in his car, he stands just outside Roberta's bedroom window singing

Top Forty. Sometimes Roberta would like to drop a stone on him from her second-floor window, plop it on his head like a dollop of bird shit, a warning to shut up. But she suspects Frank is immune to warnings. Besides, he has epileptic fits, and the neighbors feel sorry for him. He's had seizures on the sidewalk.

This is his story: "I used to drink a case a beer a day until I accidentally drove my truck off a bridge."

"You're lucky to be alive, Frank."

"The Lord kept me alive for a reason. Must be I'm suppose to find a wife."

Frank is overweight and doesn't seem to have a job. His eyes sag, but he never stops singing.

"Hey! Did you happen to see? The most beautiful girl? In the world?" he croons to the ladies who live on his block. As soon as he sees a woman, he gets out of his car and starts performing. Some neighbors are nice and talk to him, but others, like Roberta, cringe and dart indoors. "*Well*. If you did. Tell her. I'm. *Soorrrry*."

Roberta's noticed that Frank stops singing when Betty walks by. Betty, who slouches in her scuffed heels and ripped pantyhose, her oily hair dyed black. She's too old for short skirts, but she imagines herself a beauty. She pretends to survive.

Frank pauses until she's out of earshot. "Tell her. I'm. *Soorrry*," he sings to Roberta as she leaves for work. He routinely asks her to church.

She looks at the ground to discourage conversation; she frowns. Once she snapped, "Frank, get lost."

Frank likes to give her gifts. He has a trunk full of empty cookie tins and outdated magazines. Sometimes he tears the pages and makes paper carnations to decorate the inside of his car and tape around his rearview mirror. He makes bouquets for the ladies on his block.

"What do you think, Roberta?" Frank asks her one evening as she arrives home from work. "You're a florist. What do you think? Lifelike, huh?"

Roberta tries to refuse his decorations, but a box of gifts turns up outside her door. Lonely trinkets abandoned like a litter of kittens. This isn't the first time it's happened, that useless offerings are made in the name of love: scratched records, mismatched teacups and stale candy, an old cracker tin, a bag of plastic jewelry from a gumball machine, a stack of magazines. Most of it's junk that Roberta puts in the back alley. But once in a while she finds a keeper, a small thing.

For instance, an article she finds about pinhole cameras: she doesn't mean to read it, but she gets interested in the pictures, and then the captions. Before she knows it, she's spooning ice cream from a container and reading the whole thing.

It says that pinhole cameras are homemade and comically primitive. They lack lenses and shutters and focusing controls, yet pinholes are quite accurate and invert images inside their dark boxes. "Camera obscura," it's called. Consider this, the article says: a window is a very large pinhole, and the light that streams in is a fuzzy image of the scene outside. Just very unfocused. *What an idea!* Roberta thinks. Images entering your space without your intention, altering the way you see the world. Add film in a dark box, and you've got a pinhole recording the view for posterity.

The article says, do this: make your own camera out of anything—a cracker box, a cookie tin, an old oatmeal container. Keep it dark, the article says. Put in film. Place the pinhole camera in front of a saltshaker, a wildflower, a wedding ring, and alter these objects into Mysterious Masterpieces. Wait a long time for light to seep in. The magazine shows one man who used his mouth as a dark box and photographed the back of his teeth. Light peeps through his open lips; his mouth is the pinhole.

Roberta tapes the photo to her refrigerator door. The picture isn't clear or defined, which could be the fault of perspective, the gray fog of pinhole photographs. But then again, it's the inside of this man's mouth, the stains on the backs of his teeth, and who gets to see that very often? Maybe the dentist. Maybe if you hold a mirror a certain way.

Roberta scoops the ice cream down to the bottom of the container. These thoughts stick with her, could possibly change her life. A gift. She considers thanking Frank but never does.

Here's a Polaroid of the orthodontist's office when Roberta is fourteen. There she is, thin and homely with her mouth wide open while Dr. Trout leans over her. He grips the needle-nose pliers and yanks at the metal on her teeth, as if he's caught a stubborn fish and is trying to pull the hook out. Roberta counts the drop tiles on the ceiling and wonders if Dr. Trout is having an affair with the hygienist, the way their heads cock together while their hands are in her mouth. The hygienist slips with a tool and stabs Roberta's gum. "Oh, I'm sorry," the woman says.

"Aha-hhah," Roberta tries to answer, but cannot make them understand. Her poor, wide-open mouth, where everything but words fit in. Blame it on the suction hose that slurps her saliva dry and drains the vocabulary right out of her.

"We're going to make you look like a movie star," Dr. Trout promises. Roberta doesn't know whether she can believe a man who smells of too much aftershave, but she wishes it were so, if only to attract a boy in her science class named Clyde. Dr. Trout adjusts the light above him to shine directly in her mouth. It is the only spotlight aimed directly at her. He tightens and readjusts her braces, and afterward gives her several sticks of wax and packs of rubber bands to tie her mouth together. All of this to transform her into a beauty. That's the great hope.

"They're going to want you in Hollywood!" he promises and winks at Roberta's mother, who stands at the appointment desk with her pocketbook in hand.

"Hollywood. I certainly hope so," her mother says as she digs through her belongings, pulling everything out, lipstick and keys, before finding her checkbook. "This poor child needs something. We don't want her to be a wallflower her whole life, do we?" She smiles at Roberta and pinches her cheek, tries to fix her hair.

Roberta slouches and stares into a fishbowl on the counter filled with plastic bracelets and fake pearls. She reaches into the bowl and pulls out a plastic diamond ring, shoves it in her pocket for later.

Then the office door opens and Clyde walks in, just like in the movies. Roberta parts her bangs and smiles, but her upper lip gets caught on her braces. She's aware of every ounce of herself as the hygienist hustles Clyde down the hall.

"Hi, Clyde," Roberta says too late, in a whisper, her mouth dry and sore, all the sound sucked out of her.

These are her early experiences with love, pretty average as these things go.

At school, she draws hearts in her notebook and stares at the back of Clyde's head during science. Other than seeing Clyde, Roberta doesn't like science very much. Continental drift and so on. The microscopic process of things shifting, of water smoothing rocks, of billions of years going by. At fourteen, Roberta isn't interested in unmeasurables. The only continental drift she cares to understand is the achingly slow motion of her teeth squeezing into place. She wants a standard measure to define the amount of time it will take for Clyde to notice her, or an equation that'll tell her when to give up. (For many years, she struggles to understand the guiding principles of love: if only it were possible to live one's life strictly according to the laws of math and science, if only there was one answer and it made sense.)

At night, she dreams about Clyde when she rubs Ambesol on the sore spots in her mouth. She rolls little wax balls to put on the wires that stick out and jab her cheek. She's never kissed a boy, but she longs to kiss Clyde, though when she envisions it, the picture in her head gets distorted. Somehow her braces lock with Clyde's braces and they're stuck, unable to kiss or speak, or part. Roberta would almost prefer to puncture herself on a rusty old tin can and contract lockjaw than to endure an embarrassment like that.

"Moon, moon, moon," she sings. "Speak to me sooooon!" She makes up her own verse. Years later she'll sit on her bedroom floor surrounded by wadded tissues and belt out the wrong words to her favorite song.

Even as time passes and the temptation to make phone calls to her ex-lover, "just to be friends," leaves her, she continues to watch her neighbors across the alley through their curtainless windows. They're like fish swimming in a box of fluorescent light. She views their life as a photograph: a still life, a stuck life, lit from the inside out. Roberta sits on her fire escape in the shadows where she can see them clearly, two people not saying much.

The man stands tall and thin in his jockey shorts and plays the saxophone. His sheet music is held to the refrigerator door by magnets. Roberta watches while he blows his sax as if he's playing to a packed crowd, the crowd of condiments inside the door. He doesn't play with much passion, but he can sight read. He begins each song a few times, determined to make it all the way through. False starts of "Moonglow," "I Got It Bad," or "Begin the Beguine."

The wife sits at the kitchen table, flipping through magazines while he plays. A metronome rests on the windowsill. Roberta imagines the wife bought it for him, that she was tired of all the false starts and pieces of music caught between wrong notes, that she wanted to hum along but couldn't follow a song to the end. Roberta also credits the wife for realizing the thing missing from her husband's music was consistency, a steady beat.

"Happy birthday," the wife said one day and handed him a pink package.

"Thank you," he answered. He unwrapped the metronome and wound the key. Then he sat the metronome on the table while the two of them stood side by side and watched the dainty arm rock back and forth.

This is a scene Roberta envies, evidence of a charming love. She forgets that it never actually took place, that it's just another of her imagined conversations.

Roberta has conversations that go nowhere. Dialogues with the Looking Glass: words she wishes she'd said at the time, or words she plans to use.

"Yes, I'm a florist," she says. "I'm commissioned to do arrangements for some of the most exclusive events in town," she brags.

"Oh, my," someone will say. They'll admire her. "I bet you see some interesting places! Old mansions and cathedrals!"

"Well, yes," she sighs, she answers herself. "After a while you get used to it, all the glamour, all the brides…how beautiful everything is, knowing in small part you had something to do with it." She puckers her lips to the mirror and kisses the air to check her lipstick. She's curled her hair, drawn eyeliner and sparkling blue shadow across the hoods of her eyes and put on her best padded bra. She's dressing for her twenty-fifth high school reunion, trying on clothes for the mirror. Roberta smiles at herself and winks. She plans to avoid all direct questions about her own state of marriage by standing next to the food table and eating hors d'oeuvres. "Excuse me," she'll say. She'll chew her teriyaki chicken wing and look around the room with a napkin to her mouth. She'll excuse herself to get a drink at the bar and ask someone, "Have you seen Clyde?"

At the last minute she decides not to go.

In part, it's because her early experiences at parties were flattened, graceless and overwrought; she never knew what to say. For instance, at fifteen at a sleep-over: instead of being in the club basement with the other girls, who are downstairs spinning limbo records and playing Mystery Date, Roberta's in the kitchen with her mouth wide open, waiting for her best friend's mother to finish inspecting her braces.

"Look at this!" the mother calls to her husband. "You wouldn't believe how far her teeth used to stick out!" Roberta stares at the light fixture overhead while the adults peer into the pit of her mouth and marvel at the gradual alignment of her teeth. "What a pity," she can almost hear them thinking. "Such a small, skinny child with such gigantic teeth."

Roberta imagines she is the wolf in Little Red Riding Hood. "My, what big teeth you have," the characters say dumbly, before they get eaten.

Another party, another disappointment, a coed party this time: Roberta finds herself hiding under a twin bed in the dark with a girl named Erica. This wasn't Roberta's idea, but she follows because the other girl is popular, someone to be envied. Roberta thinks it's strange that a popular girl would hide under a bed during a party, but decides it must be acceptable, a secret initiation of sorts. They wait, but no one comes to look for them so they talk about their favorite love songs and whisper about boys. Clyde's name comes up. Suddenly the other girl, Erica, moves from her hiding place. "I'm bored. I'm going back downstairs.

Don't tell anyone we were here," she whispers. "I'll go down first; you wait before coming back to the party."

When Roberta eventually sneaks downstairs again, no one notices. She stands to the side eating potato chips while the other girls sing along to a Beach Boys record. The guys punch each other and glance over at the girls. Finally, someone says, "Roberta, what's wrong with your hair? You've got dust all over your head." The girls squeal as they pick dust balls out of her hair. "Where were you?" they chide. Erica laughs along with the group and doesn't say anything.

Why does she remember these episodes now? These weren't defining moments in her life, incidents that damaged her. But the thought of her high school reunion has made her revisit some old humiliations, and as much as she practices her life for the mirror, she can't help feeling disappointed that these things still happen.

Sitting on her sofa in her dress clothes, Roberta watches TV and tries to convince herself that there is still time left to go to her reunion. But something holds her back. For the time being, it's a news program on TV in which a woman sobs about how her husband was wrongfully accused of a crime, how he's being framed. The investigative reporter seems to have some evidence to corroborate the wife's theory, and Roberta is interested to see how it turns out. She's hoping the husband isn't lying; she's almost crossing her fingers. This suspense is why Roberta tells herself she can't leave yet. She's waiting for the commercial to end so she can find out more.

Then, beneath her window, her neighbor Frank calls to her. "Hey, Roberta, come on outside and talk!" Roberta is certain she won't leave her house now, if only to avoid Frank. "Hey, Roberta, come outside. Your boyfriend's here," Frank says. She looks out the window. Frank is pretending to make out with himself. He turns his back to her, wraps his arms around himself and runs his fingers through his hair, up and down his hips. He makes kissing noises in the air. Roberta cringes.

"Frank! Go home!" she snaps, as though she's talking to a stray dog, one that won't stop humping her leg.

She knows Frank is used to it, the rejection. Frank has an apartment but sits in his broken-down Granada instead, smoking cigars and singing with the radio. He sits in his car every day, even in winter, running the engine to stay warm; in the summer, he watches the bugs gather by the streetlight and blows smoke at the mosquitoes. Sometimes an old man named John sits in the car with Frank. They listen to ball games and laugh, though John is uneasy being seen with Frank, Roberta can tell. John is friends with Frank when no one else is looking. But as soon as Frank spots a woman and gets out of his car to perform, taking the cigar from his mouth and spreading his arms wide, old John leaves. He goes inside his apartment by himself, refusing to be associated with such displays of neediness. Roberta understands perfectly. It embarrasses her, enrages her, to be caught in proximity to desperate people.

Roberta closes her curtains on Frank and goes back to the TV. On the news program, the wife is saying she doesn't know what to believe. In light of new evidence, things are slowly dawning; her perceptions are changing. Someone else, an expert, is suggesting the husband must have a mental illness to appear so loving on one hand and yet to have lied so convincingly. What is it, Roberta wonders, when you believe a thing so thoroughly, and then a day goes by and your view has changed?

There's coverage of the man's trial, but Roberta doesn't hear it all for the ruckus outside. Frank is yelling again, but this time not at her. He's screaming at Betty, who ogles him from across the street.

"Take a picture! It'll last longer!" Frank bellows. Betty gives him the finger. Old John slinks out of Frank's car. "Get out of here, you old tart!" Frank continues. "You're an insult! We don't want you!" Frank nearly blubbers. "Stop staring!" But nothing changes. Betty sits alone, trying to look as pretty as she can.

And then Roberta notices something she failed to spot before: Frank is drinking. He reaches inside his car and pulls out a beer can. He pops the lid and guzzles it, then crushes the can and throws it back into his car. He reaches for another. It slowly dawns on Roberta that these are not his first beers this evening, though certainly his first in years; she also notices that Frank is being transformed into someone more hideous than before. She almost wishes for the old Frank.

"Stop staring!" he almost cries. He becomes disorderly and rips his paper flowers from his rearview mirror. He opens his car doors and throws his empty beer cans at the light pole.

"Drunks don't interest me," Betty says and shakes her head. She shuffles away, but Frank keeps going, shouting obscenities in her direction and pounding on the hood of his car. Eventually, he passes out in the front seat, his forehead pressed against the steering wheel.

A few hours later, Roberta is disturbed by the sound of moaning. She looks outside to find Frank writhing on the sidewalk in his underwear, scraping himself raw on the cement. He's disgusting in his exposure, and Roberta is about to tell him to shut up and go inside when she hears sirens nearby, driving towards them, coming up the hill. The ambulance, its lights flashing, stops just outside her house. Paramedics get out and snap sanitized rubber gloves over their hands. Roberta guesses John knew Frank was having an epileptic seizure and called 911, though the old man is nowhere in sight.

The paramedics kneel on the ground next to Frank and try to hold him still. They put a compressor on his tongue while a couple of neighbors gather outside to watch. One of the paramedics knocks on Roberta's door. She's forced to go downstairs and greet the man, who has a clipboard with questions. He needs to know if Frank lives there, since he's just outside her door, or if he has any relatives who know his medical history, and so on. Roberta answers his questions as best she can, then stays there in her doorway, in her bathrobe, watching as the paramedics try to lift Frank and strap him onto a gurney.

A few more neighbors come outside to gawk and to socialize, and before long, it's like a party. Everyone is talking. Betty comes over and stands to the side near Roberta. They watch in silence, and Roberta is stirred by the sight of Frank; in his depleted state, she almost feels compassion for him. Then the tired old prostitute turns to Roberta and says, "How come you're not with that boyfriend anymore?"

Roberta is startled. "Well, it just didn't work out," she says, though she wonders the same thing herself.

"I used to see you together," Betty says. "He was OK."

"Yeah, well…" Roberta nods. She looks past Betty's shoulder to the crowd, trying to become interested in something else.

"I know exactly what you mean," Betty says. "Maybe you should've gotten a dog together; a dog would've helped."

"Well, Betty, it just didn't work," Roberta explains again, as if she's talking to a six-year-old.

"Your boyfriend didn't have anything wrong with him," Betty says. At this point in her life, Betty's stuck with all the limping men with giant tumors on their foreheads who have nowhere else to go for love/groping/sex/whatever. It's as though Betty is the one who needs to be consoled.

"Anyway," Roberta says. She's desperate to close her door and go inside.

Then Betty turns to someone else in the crowd and says, "He shouldn't of started drinking again."

"No, you're right, he shouldn't of," one of the neighbors says.

"I wished I would of seen it, though," someone else answers. "I thought he was a mental case."

In Frank's absence, the few days he's gone for treatment in the hospital, Roberta considers making a pinhole camera following instructions in the article he gave her. What if she took a picture of her neighbors, the people on the street, the couple across the alley? She could make a camera and let it sit on her sill for hours, let the image reveal itself on film. It could look like this: the man in his kitchen playing the saxophone, the woman at the table twirling her hair. Maybe the metronome is in the picture, too, there on the windowsill, waving its arm and keeping beat to all the wrong notes. Moving like a wagging finger, an unending reprimand. "Tsk, tsk, tsk"—the scolding of their lives, the unforgiving sound of time passing.

Or Roberta could aim the camera at the wife who sits at the table while he plays, her drink on a coaster while she flips through circulars and catalogues. Roberta imagines she's looking for kitchen curtains on sale because she knows her windows are bare, that she and her husband are exposed, trapped in a box of unflattering light.

"People might get the wrong idea about us," the husband says in between songs. He's arranging his sheet music on the freezer door with magnets.

The wife shrugs and opens the door to grab a popsicle.

"Hey!"

"Sorry."

Sad, quiet moves, a life of bare windows and broken songs, viewed another way, from a distance or upside down, might look beautiful to some, to Roberta who sits in the dark and watches the couple across the alley. They look good to her.

What if Roberta were to squint? What would she see then? A world with softer edges, something close to dreams, but not quite. Looking back at her own life from a different angle, Roberta has already been part of the couple she watches across the alley. She is the woman flipping through magazines and eating ice cream. She is alone like that, then and now, staring through the window of her own life, forgetting that it is herself she's viewing and not some other quiet soul. "I remember that," she might say.

Betty, in the alley, gazes up at Roberta, who is sitting on her fire escape. Betty looks through everyone's windows at night. She is like a cat in that regard: interested from a distance, appearing and disappearing, suddenly under foot. The tired old prostitute waves and Roberta waves back. They say nothing, though Roberta's afraid that with her simple gesture she just made an unwanted friend.

When Roberta looks back to the couple, she realizes the wife is no longer in the room, but just out of sight in another room, watching TV. A blue haze bounces off the walls while the man—dressed in underwear no one else was meant to see, underwear that's usually hidden from the rest of the world—blows his saxophone toward the invisible audience on the other side of the refrigerator door. Roberta decides not to take a picture of this. She decides to aim at something else, something in daylight.

If Roberta had gone to the reunion:

Carrots and dip, teriyaki chicken wings, people gathered in a dark room trying to recall faces. They squint at each other's nametags made of old photos from the yearbook. They secretly note who has aged and gained weight, who's improved, who's gray, who appears to be alcoholic. Some of the wives pack leftovers from the buffet to take home and make meatball sandwiches. Near the end of the night, a woman wearing gold lamé skids across the wet floor as she exits the bathroom and sprains her wrist. A few husbands bend to help the woman off the floor. The DJ stops the music for a moment, but no one was dancing anyway.

She resolves to make a camera. She finds a cracker tin in the box of gifts Frank gave her, something she had not yet thrown out. She finds a nail and a hammer and pokes a hole through the tin. She visits a photography shop, explains her idea to the clerk, and purchases some film. "The approach has everything to do with it," the clerk tells her, a skinny kid with a huge Adam's apple. "If you want a certain outcome, you're going to be disappointed," he tells her. "Take a picture of anything, and it's not going to look like that." Roberta doesn't care; she wants to see things differently, see how it turns out. If it's good, maybe she'll call it art, hang it up at work among the wreaths and greenery.

She could even point the camera at herself, stand for an hour in front of a pinhole, waiting for an image, waiting for some clarity, and what would come of it? A black-and-white photo of a woman, perhaps distorted and fuzzy around the edges—a thin woman, attractive, dark hair, a smile.

But it makes more sense when Roberta takes her camera outside and points it at her garden, at her peonies and impatiens, at the vines of ivy wrapped around itself, tangled with the other vines, the tall stems of her zinnias.

"What are you doing?" Betty says. She stands just beyond the fence and startles Roberta, who is holding the cracker box in front of her.

Roberta is reluctant to answer, but she says, "I want to take a picture of my flowers."

"Oh! Take a picture of me!" Betty says. "Pleease!" She's like a child asking for ice cream.

Roberta's impulse is to hide behind a bush and feign deafness. She could busy herself by digging in the dirt and hope this excuses her from more interaction. Maybe she could bury herself or dig her way to China and step through a hole to a place on the other side of the world.

"It's not that kind of picture," Roberta says.

"Oh," Betty says. "I see." She starts to turn away.

"All right," Roberta gives in, though she's not sure why.

Betty lights up and pokes her head through the fence. She wears plastic ruby earrings and a pink bracelet. She fixes her hair. Roberta takes the old tin cracker box and aims it at Betty. Then she removes black tape from the lensless aperture. "Stand very still," Roberta says. "Don't move for a long time. Don't talk."

It could be twenty minutes or a half hour that they wait for enough light to enter the peephole and form an image on the film. These two are an apparition no one understands: unlikely women facing each other squarely, but saying nothing.

Betty breaks the silence. "Is it done yet?" she asks.

"I don't think so. I think we need to stay like this a while longer."

"Are you going to give it to me when it's done?" Betty says. "I want to show it to my boyfriend."

Roberta pauses and stares down at her feet. She doubts Betty has a boyfriend, but she doesn't argue.

"Yeah, OK," she says, "but it won't be today; it needs to be developed."

It occurs to Roberta that she is now connected to this other woman. She's taking Betty's picture, and by doing so, she's saying something to Betty that she would never say out loud. What has been set in motion? Roberta doesn't know, but she senses it's too late. The continental drift has begun, changing the shape of the world in incremental movements, in moments impossible to take back once they're started.

"Is it too late to smile?" Betty asks.

Roberta shakes her head at the woman on the other side of the fence. "I don't know," she says.

OK, Goodbye

Let's say the first time she tries to walk out she loses her car keys in the front yard at night. She's sassy, maybe a little drunk. She tosses her keys in the air but misses them on the way back down. The next thing she knows, she and her husband and the neighbors' kids are on their hands and knees on the front lawn, feeling around for keys. Wet pieces of mowed grass stick to her legs as she crawls in the dark. She's cussing to herself and dizzy and hungry. She'd like to stay angry enough to leave once she finds her car keys, but she's also tired.

Then there's the scene outside in which the neighbors are loading their truck to move. It's a hot afternoon, and Vivie says, "You probably won't be here when I get back, so I want to say goodbye now and tell you how nice it was to have you as neighbors. I mean it—we won't ever get neighbors as good as you," and she starts to tear up.

Everyone hugs. They laugh and say, "Keep in touch."

"You keep in touch, too."

Vivie gets in her car and pulls away. She drives slowly and waves. They wave, and she honks and waves some more. At the corner she turns to go to the store, and they're out of sight.

Then, at the food store, something happens. Maybe she sees her husband's girlfriend, overhears her talking, and Vivie pieces together the news that her husband never stopped screwing around. It's a conversation she wasn't supposed to hear. At the same time, she sees a bird fly overhead through the grocery store. It flies across the aisles close to the sky of fluorescent lights, and Vivie realizes she just saw two things she wasn't supposed to see. Two apparitions, almost.

So when she comes home kind of dazed, knowing once again that her husband has lied to her, her neighbors are still moving. They're trying to drive their car onto the tow trailer behind their U-Haul, aiming to line the wheels up exactly. The wife is in the car steering, going nowhere, just struggling to line up according to her husband's direction. They wave to Vivie.

"We're almost ready to go!" they exclaim.

"Oh, have a safe trip," Vivie says. "Really, have a safe trip. And good luck in your new home."

"We'll miss you," they say.

"Write," Vivie says, "or call."

"OK, we will."

"OK. Goodbye!"

"OK. Goodbye!" They wave to each other as Vivie unloads her groceries and goes inside.

What she does is this: she puts her groceries away very neatly and becomes conscientious about the laundry or dusting or something that has to do with order. Then, as if in a dream, she grabs a brown paper bag and puts her belongings in it. Some oddities, because maybe she's drinking lightly. She throws in some underwear and her eyeliner pencil and a couple of bathing suits. Maybe she finds an old pair cowgirl boots she hasn't worn in years. She throws on a mini-skirt and blouse that fit well but don't match. She brings vitamins. She doesn't know where she's going with her bag, exactly. She doesn't know if she is leaving her husband or just going on vacation. Perhaps she'll decide as she drives. She'll go to a lake and rent a cheap cabin, a place to swim and sunbathe and think. That's her plan.

When she walks out of her house at dusk with her bag in her hands, the neighbors are still there. "Just a few last-minute things!" they say. The wife is holding the screen door while the husband carries a coat rack and umbrella stand.

"Here's your hat, what's your hurry?" the wife jokes like she's kicking her husband out the door. They wave to Vivie.

"Well, have a safe trip," Vivie says.

"Yeah, OK."

"And good luck."

"Good luck to you, too," the neighbors say, as if they know something.

"OK, goodbye," Vivie says.

"OK," they say, "goodbye."

Then Vivie starts her car and drives around the corner again and waves. She doesn't know where she's headed, but she steers north on such-and-such boulevard and stops at a light. Maybe this is where someone walks by, a woman with pink hair or something. Does Vivie have an epiphany of sorts? Probably not.

She pulls away from the light, past the bank and the liquor store, through the residential section. She starts to accelerate, but her car won't pick up speed. In fact, the car slows down. She pulls over on the side of the road.

Here's a woman who's stuck three miles away from her house with her hazard lights flashing. She sits in her car and waits, in case something more might happen. Maybe a stranger will stop to help her. Maybe she won't have to make that phone call. No one stops. She bangs the steering wheel and cries and eventually walks to someone's house to borrow their phone.

An hour later her father arrives with his pickup truck and cables and hooks her car to his. That's where she finds herself at the end of the story: behind his truck with his red hazard lights flashing in her windshield. That's all she can see. She glides behind him, not able to steer herself, and contemplates warnings and hindsight, twenty-twenty vision, etc.

It could be that her husband Don apologizes. "Well, fine, I'm sorry!" is how he puts it.

Vivie tries to leave anyway. She wants to storm out the screen door, get in her car and drive away. Very dramatic. She's had two whiskey sours from the blender and is loopy. She wants to look sexy as she leaves—swing her hips, toss her hair, and fling her purse over her shoulder. She wants him to miss her, to not think of any other woman. But it's too late for that.

Instead, she jams her hand on the door handle, which is stuck. When she finally gets the screen door open, she can't slam it because the door is connected to the frame by a pump that closes slowly. The hiss from the hydraulic is the only sound.

And when she flings her purse over her shoulder, the contents fall out. So there she is on her hands and knees in the grass, grazing in the dark for her car keys. She finds lipstick, a pen, a bottle cap, but she can't find the keys.

Kids are playing in the yard next door. "Miss Vivie?" they yell. "Did you lose something?" Pretty soon they are in the front yard too, browsing with their hands, pulling up clumps of grass. One child skims the lawn with his feet.

Don stands at the screen door and watches. He turns on the porch light, which blinds them briefly. The porch light does not help. It turns everything into shadow.

A few weeks later, when she tries to leave again, she sits in the dark and steers, turns the wheel blindly because she is being towed and cannot see anything except the red flashers of her father's taillights in front of her. Two red lights flashing for an hour, for eternity, like a warning on the way to hell. Slow down. Caution. Beware.

Vivie feels herself getting tired as she's pulled along. She's mesmerized by the rhythm of the taillights, red, black, red, black, red, black, a drumbeat without sound.

What if she decides to turn her steering wheel in a direction sideways from her father's truck? The fact is she's still connected, unable to pull away.

Don had his hand on another woman's knee. It's captured in a photograph from a recent party. He tells Vivie she's just imagining things, making them more tangled than they need to be.

"Vivie," he says, "you get yourself too upset about these things."

Usually she believes him, but this particular humid night, mosquitoes biting both of them, Vivie has a flash of clarity, despite the whiskey sours she's been drinking. She stares into the refrigerator with the door wide open, and something about the bowl of moldy potato salad makes it apparent that everything has gone bad. So she grabs her purse and tries to storm out the front door. Which is when she drops the keys.

Let's say there's another scene in the grocery store when Vivie bumps into her husband's girlfriend and pretends not to notice. She turns down a different aisle to hide, and when she wheels away, her back to the other woman, Vivie hears the girlfriend say, "That's Don's wife. He's the one I was telling you about."

"The guy you went out with the other night?" Vivie hears another voice say, but doesn't catch the answer. She isn't certain she's heard anything correctly, but she grows determined while she stacks cans of frozen fruit juice in her cart.

At the register, in a bit of a triumphant haze, she smiles at the cashier. She's not really aware of her surroundings, but is confident as she writes a check for her groceries. Then she pushes her cart out the door with her chin up, feeling beautiful and right for the first time in ages. She lets the grocery boy in his red apron follow her when she wheels her cart across the parking lot. She opens her trunk and moves aside old tennis shoes and jumper cables so the grocery boy has room to fit her bags. She is confident and will not be swayed, even when her car stalls. She is strong and does not feel the need to yield as she exits the parking lot and pulls into traffic. She has her windows rolled down, and she turns off the radio, resolved to be free from all the ways the world has bound her. Free from rules and fear and worry. Free from her husband and his half-truths. She is a bird carried by the wind, and she drives through a red light in this state, not because she means to, but because a breeze kind of pushes her that way.

But back up. In the grocery store, while she's preoccupied, Vivie catches sight of a bird. Did she just see that? A plain old bird, nothing fancy. It flies towards the BAKERY sign, where big, boxy letters protrude from the wall. The bird has a nest on the top of the K and has found things, even in the grocery store, scraps of plastic and cigarette butts and lottery tickets, enough to make a nest, to rebuild a life. Vivie smiles at the bird, at the K, for a long time.

When she gets home, Vivie can tell the neighbor's wife is not happy. "I'm trying!" the wife fumes. She's sweating inside the car, the windows rolled down, as she rocks the car forward and back several times. The husband is standing in front gesturing with his hands. "A little more to the left. OK, stop," he says. "Now back up and turn a hair to the right. Just a hair." The wife turns a hair, and Vivie hears the husband say, "No! That's too much. You turned too much." Vivie has her back to them as she leans across the trunk to unload her groceries.

"Why don't you steer it yourself!" the wife says.

The husband sighs. "Try it one more time."

"Why can't we just drive this goddamn car up on the trailer ramp? It was fine before."

"I thought we could make it better. Straighten it out some more."

Vivie has both hands loaded with plastic grocery bags. They hang from her arms like a set of scales. She closes the door with her hip.

"You're still here?" she calls to her neighbors.

"We're on our way!" the husband yells back cheerfully.

"Once we get this goddamn car back on the trailer," the wife says. "We've driven this car back and forth, back and forth, up and down the goddamn ramp." The wife leans out the car window and waves.

"Well, have a safe trip," Vivie says. She tries to wave, but her hands are full of groceries. She lifts one arm as if she's doing an arm curl and moves her fingers in her neighbor's direction, like a wave but not quite. "OK, bye," she yells. But they've already returned to the business of aligning the car with the ramp.

The sky is beautiful, a shade of dark purple blue, and off in the distance is a giant moon. A large half pie. A wide apparition. A pink, pink moon. The world is OK. Vivie will be fine. She decides it. She has the doors and windows open, and there is a perfect, humid breeze.

The breeze reminds her of a time, years ago, on a night like this, when she left Don and drove eight hours to visit a friend from high school. She stayed a week before coming home again. Since then, she's lost touch with her friend, but the mood of that evening returns every once in a while.

This is when Vivie decides to pack a paper bag full of bathing suits and vitamins. She puts on an old pair of boots.

"How many more times do I have to hear this?" Don says. "It wasn't like I went home with someone else."

"I'm just saying—" Vivie answers.

"What? So I had my hand on her goddamned knee, for Christ sake! It's a photograph! We were posing for a fucking photograph."

"Don, people will hear you, lower your voice. The kids across the street will hear you."

And she's right, she knows the neighborhood can hear them argue—maybe not all the specifics, but Don is loud and easy to understand. They can make out the words "Fuck!" and "Goddamn!" every so often.

The only way Vivie can quiet Don is by running the blender for her whiskey sours. She lets the motor whirl for longer than necessary to drown out his voice. When she thinks he's through, she turns it off and pours herself a drink. But then Don starts up again, defending himself. So Vivie turns the blender on and takes comfort in the high-pitched wail of spinning blades. Just loud enough so she can no longer hear herself think. Loud enough to overpower every thought and bring a bit of peace. Loud, angry peace.

"Don't think," she says to herself while she stares into the refrigerator, the blender still screaming in the background. "Don't think." She reaches in the fridge for the bowl of potato salad, and when she notices mold growing around the sides of it she throws it in the trash, bowl and all. She throws away some runny lettuce and a ham carcass, too.

This doesn't solve her immediate problem, though. The freezer is empty, and she's hungry. She decides she'll storm out of the house, pretend she's leaving him, when really she'll go to the store for ice cream.

So she grabs her purse and jams her hand on the screen door which doesn't slam, and swings her hips as she walks out. The blender still whirls in the kitchen. The house is a circus of lights and sounds, and she's ditching it.

Then Vivie spills her purse and loses her keys, and the circus continues outside on her front lawn. The neighborhood kids roam her yard in their bare feet, and Don stands at the screen door turning the porch light on and off like he's signaling a warning or speaking in Morse code (Save Our Ship), the lights bright and dark, bright and dark in a weird arrhythmic strobe. Vivie sits in the grass, stunned. She'd like to disappear from this scene. Instead, she's witness to the funhouse of her life, a disturbing world of dwarves and giants sorting themselves out in her front yard. "I found it!" one child says.

"No, that's not it, you dork."

"Hey, turn the lights back on, we can't see!"

So it's another night with a pink moon and a humid breeze when Vivie gets stuck by the side of the road with her hazards flashing. Her father, when he comes to get her, is older, a thin man with gray hair. He stretches on the ground to fiddle with the underside of her bumper, fastening things to other things Vivie will never understand. Her father works with the quiet sureness he has always had, and Vivie notices how they've both gotten older.

She stands by the side of the car, her shoulders drooped, her hands at her side and her feet slightly parted, just as she did when she was ten years old, watching her father shoot rabbits or cuss flat tires.

Or maybe she doesn't remember this exactly. She just has the sensation of standing in the same posture as when she was ten, unable to understand, even years later, what she feels in her father's presence.

While she's being towed and red and black and red and black and red are the only things she sees, she thinks, "This is one more instance of I don't know what."

But let's say, when her engine dies, she tries to think of a way to get out of this jam on her own. She imagines someone stopping to help her, someone handsome who'll fix her car and wish her well as she drives away. But she'd rather not rely on a man to save her, especially not her husband—but any man, really, including the stranger in her head, or her father.

Maybe this is when she sees the girl with bright pink hair. Could be pink dreadlocks wrapped in an orange scarf, a lovely nest of matted hair. Could be the apparition of a beautiful girl with pink hair, or the combination of pink and orange that reminds Vivie of something exotic and free.

"Would a girl with pink hair have car troubles?" Vivie wonders. It seems a ridiculous question, but as she watches the girl with dark eyes and straight posture, she figures the answer is no. No, she wouldn't have car troubles in quite the same way. Perhaps she'd get stuck leaving a husband one day, too. But Vivie doubts she'd sit inside her vehicle with the windows rolled up, wondering whom to call, husband or father. A girl with pink hair would get out of the car, grab her suitcase, and walk.

Vivie falls in love with the girl. She envies her as the girl crosses the intersection without waiting for the light. A car speeds by, just missing her, and honks. A crow caws overhead. Vivie bites her thumbnail and watches in case something more happens. The girl with pink hair doesn't turn around. She walks past Vivie's car, the hazard lights flashing, and doesn't turn to look. Vivie glances in the rearview mirror to check her own hair and lipstick, and then looks back at the girl who's walking away.

Acknowledgments

Most of the stories in this collection were previously published in somewhat different form in the following journals:

The Sun: "My Life as a Mermaid"; *City Sages: Baltimore:* "Joe Blow"; *Other Voices:* "What Girls Leave Behind"; *Sententia:* "Still at War" (as "Injured"); *Little Patuxent Review:* "End of August"; *Hunger Mountain:* "I Get There Late"; *[PANK]*'s blog: "Lawrence Loves Somebody on Pratt Street"; *Blue Earth Review:* "Stray"; *GSU Review:* "Small Deaths"; *Indiana Review:* "OK, Goodbye."

My sincere thanks to the following people for their friendship, encouragement and great editorial feedback on earlier versions of these stories: Mary Jo LoBello Jerome, Rosemary Berkeley, Lisa Lynn Biggar, Guy Thorvaldsen, François Camoin, Diane Lefer, David Jauss, Rafael Alvarez, Laura Shovan, Gina Frangello, Rupert Wondolowski, Betsy Boyd, and Jen Michalski. Special thanks and deep appreciation to Paula Bomer.

Also, big thanks to Steven Gillis, Dan Wickett, Guy Intoci, Michelle Dotter and everyone at Dzanc Books for believing in my work.

Thanks to Dad, Mom, Jim and my entire family, immediate and extended, for your love and support.

Finally, and most especially, thanks to Lee for your understanding and patience and your great big generous heart.